D0252572

DIAMOND DOGS

DIAMOND DOGS

A NOVEL

Alan Watt

LITTLE, BROWN AND COMPANY

Boston   New York   London

AUTHOR'S NOTE

Diamond Dogs is the title of an early seventies David Bowie album.
There is no connection between this story and David Bowie or his album.

First Edition

The characters and events in this book are fictitious.
Any similarity to real persons, living or dead, is coincidental
and not intended by the author.

Library of Congress Cataloging-in-Publication Data
Watt, Alan.
Diamond dogs : a novel / Alan Watt — 1st ed.
p.   cm.
ISBN 0-316-92581-0
1. Fathers and sons — Fiction.   2. Teenage boys — Fiction.
3. Sheriffs — Fiction.   4. Nevada — Fiction.   I. Title.
PR9199.3.W3796 D5   2000
813'.6 — dc21
00-025224

10   9   8   7   6   5   4   3   2   1

Designed by Steve Dyer
Q-FF
Printed in the United States of America

To my mother and father

There is no greater illusion than fear.

— *Tao Te Ching*

DIAMOND DOGS

SUNDAY NIGHT

1

I WAS ANGRY. We were all at Fred Billings's house. He lived in a farmhouse on the outskirts of Carmen. His father raised chickens. The whole place stank of chickens. He let them run around in this corral that he surrounded with a mesh-wire fence. I liked that about Fred's father. He could have made a lot more money if he'd kept those chickens in cages and fed them that low-grade steroid shit, but instead he let them run free.

Mr. Billings had gone into Las Vegas with his wife to see Dorothy Hamill in *Enter the Night,* so Fred decided to have a party. It was mostly the football team. They were all downstairs getting wasted or outside sitting by the fire. We always ended up at Fred's house. It wasn't the most convenient place to get to, it wasn't even all that nice, but Fred's folks never hassled us so that's where we ended up.

Fred played center. He was big and wide, his forehead

was this beefy ridge of flesh, and he had an irreparable underbite. I don't know anything about genetics, but judging by his folks Fred was not going to age well. It was hard to believe that this was as good-looking as he was going to get.

His girlfriend was Amy, small and thin with large breasts, a little girl in a woman's body. She only had one eye. When she was six her father was setting off firecrackers in a coffee can and the whole mess blew up in her eye. The doctors replaced it with a blue glass iris that didn't quite match, but she was still pretty cute, and Fred was crazy about her.

I was up in Fred's parents' bedroom with my girlfriend, Lenore. I had her shirt off and my mouth wrapped around one of her big brown nipples. I was trying to get my hands down her shorts, but she kept grabbing them and putting them back on her tits. This had been going on for a while, I mean like over a year, and that's why I was starting to get angry.

"I can't," she said.

I had my jeans around my ankles and my dick straining to Jupiter. She touched it for a second, her long, soft fingers running up the base while I held my breath. And then she stopped. My mind was racing, searching for the right words to make her continue, but the best I could come up with was *More.*

"I can't."

I got off the bed and started to pull on my jeans.

"What's wrong?"

6

"I can't do this anymore," I said.

"Do what?"

"Not have sex, that's what."

And then she started to cry. I never knew what to do when she cried, I just stood there feeling guilty and out of control. She kept telling me that it wasn't *personal*, like if I'd been someone else she still wouldn't have wanted to have sex with me. I didn't know why she was talking about not having sex with someone else. I *wanted* it to be personal. My head was spinning and so I went into the bathroom. I was staring at myself in the mirror and thinking about jerking off when I heard a knock at the door.

"What do you want?"

"What's the matter with Lenore?" It was Reed, my best friend.

"I don't know."

"She's crying, man." I wanted him to go away. "What are you doing in there?"

I opened the door. Reed was drunk; he had two beers in his hands, and he handed me one. He was looking at me with this wide-eyed expression.

"This is our year, man. This is it. We're going . . . we're fuckin' going . . . fuckin' all the way!"

He was hugging me. I still had some of my erection left so I stuck my butt out in case he noticed. He was practically sobbing. He got very emotional when he talked about football. I almost felt like crying too, but I couldn't, it wasn't something that my father encouraged. He took it personally. I didn't understand that before, but now I do. It was just too much for him.

Reed's family had moved to Carmen from Bakersfield when he was eight. He'd walked into the classroom in the middle of the school year looking tough and scared. He sat at the back of the class while all of the kids watched him, gawking. Except for me. I kept my eyes on the board, pretending to pay attention, and then at recess I followed him out to the far end of the field.

"Hey."

"Hey."

"Where the hell's Bakersfield?"

"California."

"How come you moved here?"

"My daddy's a mechanic, he took a job here with his brother-in-law." Reed didn't talk like the rest of us; his speech was slow, and when he spoke his eyes wandered all over your face like they were searching for a place to land. I felt this pounding inside of me, but I was scared and so I asked him if he wanted to fight. He said that he would if I wanted to but he'd rather race me back to the school. And so we raced. He led all the way. I kept running, hoping that he would tire, but he didn't. He beat me by twenty yards. Between gasps he told me, "I was . . . the fastest . . . runner at . . . my last . . . school."

As we walked back into the school I noticed that our strides matched perfectly. With most people you're either a little ahead or a little behind, until eventually you're not even on the same street anymore — but walking with Reed was effortless, it was one of those things that I just never even had to think about.

We finished our beers and went downstairs. Lenore was standing by the kitchen door talking to Amy. When she saw me she turned away. Amy took her hand and pulled her into the kitchen. It drove me crazy when I knew that somebody was talking about me behind my back, especially a girl. Girls could make anything that a guy did sound bad. Once Paula Bell told us about some guy who liked her and one time while he was laughing snot came out his nose and landed on her dress. It was an accident, but the way she told it made him sound so pathetic that we all started calling him Snot.

I can't even remember his name, I just remember Snot. I always wanted to apologize to him, explain to him that I didn't mean it, but I never did. Sometimes I think that if I'd had the guts to apologize to him then maybe this whole thing would never have happened. I don't know, maybe it was inevitable — maybe what happened had nothing to do with guts.

There was a lot of noise coming from the living room. D. J. Farby was lying on his back on the floor while Craig Nutt and Benny Jericho funneled beer into his mouth from a plastic boot. When they saw me they all screamed, "Garvin!"

I kept my throat open and let the beer flow right into my stomach without taking a breath. If you took a breath you could drown. I lay there and felt the alcohol hit me; the whole back of my head went warm, and for a few seconds I didn't feel angry anymore. My eyes felt as if they were floating around in their sockets, about to come loose. I just lay there on my back listening to Nirvana blaring from the stereo.

"You sick fuck!" hollered the Penguin, our stumpy half-back. His name was Craig Nutt, but he had a long torso with tiny arms and legs so we called him the Penguin.

I stood up and the room started spinning. Benny and the Penguin steadied me and I think I told them I loved them. I prowled the room, screaming along with Kurt Cobain, making up my own lyrics:

> I'm a screamer, you're a bleeder,
> You're a squealer, I'm your dealer!

Nothing mattered. Everybody was drunk, the music was blasting, and we all felt invincible. I passed the front window and that was when I saw these two skinny freshmen walking up Fred Billings's driveway toward the house. One was blond and the other had black hair. I don't even remember how it happened, I just remember being outside and having the blond one in a headlock while Blackie, his knees knocking together, watched from a safe distance.

Blackie was skin and bone, probably tipped the scale at ninety pounds. I remembered seeing him in the cafeteria.

All the jocks sat together, laughing loud and shoving each other, and Blackie sat with his friends, looking over at us with this dark, frightened look like he was missing something special.

Somebody always smashed a plate at lunchtime. It was a daily tradition at our table. Whoever did it would act horrified, and if it was the Penguin he'd pretend he was crying as the teacher rushed over, prepared to give us hell. They'd make rules like the next person who dropped a plate would get detentions for a week, but it never happened. Everybody would be clapping and laughing and we were the center of attention.

One day Blackie dropped his plate. He was walking past our table and suddenly we all heard this crash. Everyone started whooping and screaming, except for us. Blackie was grinning. He'd done it on purpose. The rest of the school turned to us for their cue and when they saw that we weren't applauding they stopped almost instantly. It got very quiet — Blackie was standing there all alone picking up his broken plate while his grin turned to panic. And then somebody yelled out, "He wet his pants!" I don't think he actually did, it was probably his apple juice that spilled, but it made a perfect stain down his leg and everybody started chanting, *PISS, PISS, PISS, PISS, PISS!* He picked up the rest of his lunch, put it on his tray, and threw it into the garbage. We kept chanting until he was well out of the cafeteria and far out of earshot, but after something like that you're never out of earshot.

*   *   *

I was holding Blondie's face in the dirt and making him say, "I want my mommy." He had to say it twenty times before I let him go, but after he said it seventeen times, I kept repeating, "Seventeen."

"That was twenty," he said.

I asked him, "Whose face is in the dirt?"

"Mine," he said. And that was when I felt the beer leave me. I didn't feel drunk anymore. I was just watching myself holding this kid's face on the ground and all I could think about was my father.

That night I'd asked my father if I could borrow his car. He drove a mint-condition '67 Eldorado; it was a color that I'd never seen in the desert before, a color that for the longest time I couldn't place. It was the color of rust. He looked up at me from his chair, spun the cubes of ice in his glass, and said, "What are you going to do for me?" His eyes were blurry and he had this curled-up half-smile.

"What do you mean?"

"What do I mean." He stared at the television. "I mean what are you going to do for me?"

"What do you want?"

There was a sleeping-pill commercial on the television that had the pill singing about how it would knock you out cold and you'd wake up refreshed. "I want you to sing."

I stared at the floor. I didn't feel like singing, I just wanted to get out of the house. "I thought you meant like a chore or something."

"No. I want you to sing that commercial."

I felt my throat go dry; I tried to say that I didn't know the words but all that came out was air. All I said was, ". . . words."

"What?"

"I don't know the words."

And then he roared with laughter. "Make 'em up."

I sang for a minute. He just sat there and stared at the television with his finger on the mute button. He didn't laugh. He didn't make a sound. I stopped for a second but he said, "Minute's not up yet." And so I kept singing. For a full minute I sang, making up words, hating him, hating myself, but singing because I knew that he would give me the keys to his car.

I'd traded places with the Penguin. Now he was holding Blondie by the ankles and swinging him around in circles in the Billingses' front yard while I gave Blackie a wedgie. He was begging me to stop. Most of the girls rolled their eyes and went inside but a few of them watched and chatted with some of the other guys. Blackie was whimpering, pleading for me to stop, but I couldn't. The more he whimpered, the more I just wanted to continue; it was only after the Penguin got tired of spinning Blondie that I knew I was going to have to stop, and I felt despair.

I remember them running down Fred's driveway, their skinny legs flying over the gravel, Blackie's underwear halfway up his back and trying to pull it back down while Blondie screamed at him to "Run!" I threw a beer bottle in their direction just to hear it smash. I wanted to drown out the noise of my father's laughter as he handed me the keys and told me to get the hell out of his house.

I remember trying to push Ernie Gates into the fire. Everybody was laughing but I wasn't fooling around; I had him in a bear hug and I was dragging him toward the flames. He jabbed his elbow into my ribs. It was the kind of jab I knew was really going to hurt the next day, but that night I couldn't feel a thing, I was spinning out of control. Like Reed said, this was our year, I was the first-string quarterback for Carmen High, I had the best arm in Nevada, and this year we were going all the way.

I remember punching Ernie in the face with my fist and his nose starting to bleed.

I remember telling Fred that he should mind his own business and to go fuck his Cyclops.

I remember them holding me down and telling me to cool off.

I remember Reed yelling at them not to hurt my arm.

I remember vomiting and Reed rubbing my back and telling me to "Chill. Just chill, buddy. Everything's cool."

I remember telling them all to go fuck themselves. "Just leave me alone. I want to be alone!" But I didn't, really. I didn't want to be alone.

I was three when she walked out on us. Just threw everything into a bag and split, and all that was left was a photograph. She had jet-black hair, clear green eyes, long, muscular legs, and a dazzling smile. She danced the midnight show at the Sands. That's where my father met her —

swept her off her feet, I'm sure. But that was a long time ago.

In the photograph my mother is smiling; her hands are under my arms and she's holding me up. My father has his arm around her and a goofy grin on his face. The picture made no sense to me. He was not that man, I was not that boy, and that woman would never have left her son. I used to stare at the picture with my thumb covering my father and wait for her to come home and save me. I knew why she'd left; I just didn't understand why she hadn't taken me with her, I didn't understand how she could have left me with him.

The only memory I had of my mother was her pantyhose. We were in the laundry room and I was watching her fold her pantyhose and she was looking right at me, but her face was a blur. No matter how hard I tried, I could never see her face. And I remembered her perfume. I remembered the day that Lenore wore it to school. I told her that she shouldn't wear it, that it smelled awful and it didn't suit her body chemistry. That's what I said. And then I avoided her for the rest of the day. After practice she waited for me outside the dressing room, so I climbed out the window and hitched a ride home.

When I was five, for my birthday, my mother sent me a card and a calendar with horses. I never took it out of the plastic. I remember my father getting angry with me because I wouldn't open it. I wanted to keep it clean, show it to her when she came home, show her that I was a good boy and that I kept things clean. That was the only thing she ever sent me.

The next year, my father gave me a football. When he threw the ball with me he was a different person, he was kind and patient. When I dropped the ball he never yelled — he just chuckled and we'd try it again. We'd throw the ball around for hours and then he'd put his hand on my shoulder and we'd walk back to the house. His hands were huge, like bear claws, the fingers thick and muscular — a flick from his fingers would sting my head for days. I was terrified of my father's hands. I have my mother's hands: they're narrow, my fingers thin and bony.

I remember staggering out into the field behind Fred's house. Even then I knew I had a secret. I didn't know what it was but I knew it was awful and I just wanted to get away — away from the fire and the noise, away from everybody who seemed to be OK. I knew that I didn't belong, and that was all I wanted — to be safe, to know for just a moment what it was like to not be afraid. And so I staggered out into the field; my shirt was ripped, my hands were cut, my ribs were starting to ache, and all I could think about was how much I wanted my mother to come and take me away.

2

THEY DIDN'T WANT ME to drive home. I was sitting behind the wheel of my father's car with the windows up and the doors locked. Reed stood pleading with me through the glass but I just sat there gripping the wheel, feeling the sharp twist where my father had bent it by squeezing it too tightly.

"Just come in and have a coffee," Fred urged me from the passenger side. Benny and the Penguin stood in front of the car with their arms folded, like if I was going to drive drunk I'd have to drive through them first. They looked ridiculous, standing there prepared to die so that I wouldn't run over some stranger. I started to laugh. Mrs. Aemes, our English teacher, was always pointing out examples of "wonderful irony," and I just knew she would have had a field day with this one. I put the car into neutral and floored it and they both jumped out of the way. I tore up the gravel on Fred's father's driveway and fishtailed out into the night.

The road into Carmen was the greatest stretch of road on Earth. During the day it was nothing, just a sea of blown-out tires littered along the side of the road. The heat would get so intense on the asphalt that tires would often just melt and explode. But at night it was this long, dark corridor with no end in sight, and in your rearview mirror were the bright lights of Las Vegas, this twinkling oasis built in the middle of nowhere, built on hope. And I'd be driving away from it as fast as I could, with the cool night air blowing through my hair and Nirvana blasting from my father's CD player.

I loved Nirvana. I loved them for all the reasons my father hated them. He said you couldn't understand the words because all Kurt Cobain did was scream. My favorite song was the hidden track at the end of *Nevermind.* It just suddenly kicked in after around ten minutes of silence with this buzzy feedback and crunchy guitar and when he started singing you couldn't understand a thing he was saying. He just screamed and screamed until he was too tired to scream anymore, and then he just let his guitar scream. I wanted to scream like that, I wanted to scream like Kurt Cobain, but instead I gave people wedgies.

I was playing chicken with the headlights. I'd turn them off and see how long I could drive in total darkness. It was as if I were floating, totally free, like nothing could hurt me, like I didn't exist. With the noise and the darkness and the cool air on my face I knew that I could do anything. As long as I didn't have to think about where I was going. As long as I didn't have to think about my father.

I never knew who he was going to be. Sometimes he could be a real gentleman. On Sundays he always got to church early to hold the door open for the old ladies. He'd just stand there looking spiffy, charming the hell out of all the blue-haired relics like he was running for mayor of Nazareth. He was always flirting with the old ladies, telling them how nice they looked, and I honestly think he meant it. He was two different people, my father, and I never knew which one to expect.

Playing chicken, I'd drive in darkness as long as I could stand it, until the rush became unbearable, and then I'd turn on the lights just before I went flying off the road. I'd straighten out the car, get it back on the right side of the road, and then kill the lights again. It was during one of those dark times that I heard a thud and felt something fly off the front bumper.

At first I thought it was a stray dog; there are hundreds of them roaming around the outskirts of Carmen. People drive by and just dump them out of their cars, abandon them to roam the desert. Sometimes they breed with wolves. They just roam around, ragged and bloody, scavenging for food.

I hit the lights and slammed on the brakes. I turned the car around and shone the high-beams to see what I'd hit. It took me a couple of minutes. I had the brights on, scanning the side of the road, and then I saw him, way off, lying right next to a cactus, perfectly still, like he'd been there forever. I saw his black hair and I knew immediately who it was. And I knew he was dead.

My father was like a brick wall, a giant with a face of granite, almost cartoon-handsome until you got close to his eyes and saw the strain. They were a piercing blue that stared right through you, with this faraway look like he was amused by something that no one else could see, like he was in on some joke with a horribly tragic punch line.

He'd move quietly around the house doing whatever he needed to do — getting a cup of coffee, sorting through the mail, cleaning his gun. And then I'd hear him twist the cap off his bottle and that was when I'd know it was time to climb the stairs to my room and close the door behind me. I would sit on my bed and wait. And most of the time nothing would happen.

I looked around to see if there was any oncoming traffic. I could say that it was because I was looking for help, and maybe a part of me was, but I doubt it. I felt relief that I was alone. I jumped out of the car and went over to him. I don't know why but I started speaking to him, my voice shaking.

"Hey . . . hey, can you hear me?"

He was lying on his side in an awkward position. One of his legs had flown up over his head. I didn't want to touch him, but I put my hand on his shoulder.

"Hey, wake up." I told him to wake up.

I took his wrist and tried to find a pulse even though I

knew he was dead. I noticed that his underwear was no longer stretched up his back. I felt weak inside. I wanted to tell him that I was sorry. I wanted to explain to him that I hadn't meant to do it, any of it. For a second I even thought about pulling his leg back down. I knew it wouldn't make a difference, but I wanted to fix him. I just couldn't stand looking at him all twisted up like that and knowing that I was responsible.

Everything became quiet. All I could hear was the car humming. The music was off and for a moment I felt peaceful. I looked up at the sky and I saw a million stars. And then something happened that I can't really explain; all I know is that I felt this surge. I don't believe in God or spirits or anything but it was like this energy force just flew up and over my head and it was gone. And I was staring at a corpse. And that was when I realized what I'd done.

A truck was approaching in the distance, coming from Carmen, two minutes away. I stood there cursing myself. And cursing this kid. I started yelling at him, "You stupid shit, what were you doing?" I don't know why I was mad at him, but I was.

The truck was getting closer. It was heading out of Carmen, toward Las Vegas. I reached down and took the kid in my arms and carried him toward the car. I didn't know what I was going to do, but I knew that I couldn't leave him there in the desert. I rested his body against the bumper, pulled the keys out of my jeans, and opened the trunk. I dropped the body into the trunk, slammed it shut, and pretended that I was taking a piss on the side of the road.

There was another car approaching now, heading in my direction. I got into my father's car and pounded the accelerator, sending the tires spinning, shooting gravel into the desert.

I was starting to shiver. I put the window up and turned the heat on full blast. I couldn't stop my teeth from chattering. I wanted to pull over and think but the car behind me was getting closer. And that was when I started to pray; I don't know why, I don't believe in God, but I didn't know what else to do.

"Oh God, please God, I just want to get home. . . ."

My father's house is at the end of a very long lane. He built it back there so he could avoid the noise of traffic on the road. If he was up, I didn't know what I was going to do. Sometimes after work he'd get drunk and go to bed with Kimmy. Kimmy was his live-in lady friend. She used to be a stripper in Vegas, but after she moved in with my father she got a job working for the city of Carmen as a secretary. We used to talk once in a while when she first started going out with my father. She'd tease me about having to approve of my girlfriends and it was sort of like having a big sister, but after she moved in it seemed like all she did was chainsmoke and watch television. It was the only way she could put up with my father, she said. She'd sit in this partially constructed addition next to the dining room while my father sat in the living room listening to Neil Diamond on his stereo.

DIAMOND DOGS

My father listened to Neil Diamond night and day. I mean, very occasionally he might listen to regular radio, but regular radio in Clarke County is pretty awful, even for an older person. It's mostly that "new country" cowshit. It's insulting. I mean, at least with old country it's honest — these wrinkled old guys singing about how their wives left them and now they're broke and living in their trucks. But with new country, they're all young and beautiful and singing about the exact same problems.

Anyway, my father had every recording that Neil Diamond ever made. He'd seen him in concert a million times. Either he'd take me or one of his girlfriends or sometimes he'd just go by himself. At night he'd sit there on his leather chair, staring off into space, balancing a crystal glass of Midori on his knee, and listen to Neil. And every once in a while his lips would move along to the words.

That's what my father drank. Midori. It was this electric-green melon liqueur that bathing beauties would drink around the pool at Caesar's Palace. My father loved it. Sometimes he'd blend it with tequila and mix up a pitcher of margaritas, but most of the time he'd just pour it over ice and drink it with a little club soda. His body would relax and he'd sink deeper into his chair and he would be at peace. Sometimes he'd fall asleep, and other times he'd walk around getting increasingly irritated and then pick a fight with Kimmy. He'd get on her about her smoking too much and then she'd say something about his drinking and that would be it, they could go all night. He'd get rough with her but he'd never hit her, just grab her wrists and hold her until there wasn't much she could do but scream.

My father had a violent temper. Things were always breaking when he was around. Sometimes he'd brag to me that he'd never hit a woman: "No matter how crazy they make you, any man who hits a woman is no man." One time he got wasted and he threw Kimmy's ashtray at the mirror, smashing it. He told me to clean it up. The next day I saw him standing in the front room staring at where the mirror used to be with a puzzled expression on his face. He went to the garage and got a hammer. He yanked the nail out of the wall and filled the hole with putty, and he never asked what happened to the mirror.

He'd hit me. Smack me in the head. He wouldn't punch me, but he could smack pretty hard. He had a big silver football ring on his right hand and when it connected with my head it stung like hell.

I always knew when he was getting angry. When he was a boy, some kid had thrown a rock at him. It'd hit him on his forehead above his right eye. After it healed it left a hard little bump that when he got angry would turn bright red.

I had my foot to the floor and the needle buried but the car behind me was catching up. It was flashing its brights at me. I didn't want to pull over, but I had no choice; it would have been more suspicious if I'd kept driving. I hit the brakes and edged my father's car to the side of the road. It was Reed. He pulled up alongside me. I took a deep breath and wound down the window. Reed was already in midsentence: ". . . trying to tell you to pull over!"

"What?"

"You left your hat back at Fred's —" And then he stopped talking. He was staring at me, his eyes wide, terrified. I realized that I was shivering. My teeth were chattering and I couldn't stop them. "You left your hat at Fred's." He threw my hat through the open window. I caught it and put it back on. The team had had these yellow hats made that said CARMEN FOOTBALL on the front of them in block letters. Lenore had taken mine and sewn my jersey number, 37, onto the back in royal blue. We all wore our hats backwards, I don't know why; it created this odd-looking tan line when we took them off, a lily-white line across our foreheads from the leather band. It looked weird at first, but pretty soon almost every guy at school had a white line on his forehead, and it became a status symbol. Pretty soon, if you didn't have a lily-white line across your forehead you were getting wedgies from all over the place.

And so Reed was delivering my hat. He was looking at me with this worried look. "That was fucked up back there."

"I know."

He was just staring at me with this quizzical expression.

"Hey look, I gotta get home. I gotta get my old man's wheels back."

Reed was the best listener I had ever met. He was listening to you even when you weren't speaking, and it could get unnerving, especially if you had a secret. He could draw a secret out of you and it was like he didn't even know he was doing it. He was the sort of person that you just wanted to confide in — when you told him a story, his face reacted in all the right places.

I said it again. "I gotta go." I knew I was hurting his feelings but I didn't know what else to do.

He nodded and muttered "OK," then threw his car into gear and drove off. I watched him drive away. I waited until he made a left down Imperial Road before I began to move.

I turned off my headlights as I drove up my father's laneway. I could see the house. All the lights were off. I pulled into the garage and twisted the key and sat there listening to the silence, wondering what to do.

3

WHEN WE WENT to Las Vegas, my father transformed into a different person. He got really excited. He'd crack these corny jokes that he'd heard on *An Evening at the Improv.* One time we were eating dinner before going to see Neil Diamond and he had an artichoke on the end of his fork. He looked at it for a second and said, "You may have choked Artie, but you're not choking Chester." That was my father's name, Chester.

Driving into Vegas he'd poke me in the ribs and tell me I was growing like a weed. I was pretty tall, though not as tall as he was. I was long and skinny. Coach Ulster had me on this special diet to put some weight on me, and it was starting to work. For the last six months I'd been eating lots of red meat. My father hardly ever grumbled about it. Usually he was very cheap, but he wanted me to play football even more than I wanted it. He was always bragging about me to

27

everybody. I think most people thought he was just this charming guy who really loved his son. He hardly showed his other side, at least not outside the house. It made me wonder about everybody else. It made me wonder sometimes if everybody was a liar.

My father always dressed up for Neil Diamond. He'd spend an hour in the bathroom, oiling his hair, shaving and after-shaving, picking the hairs from his nose with tweezers. I used to sit on the toilet seat and watch him. He didn't mind. He didn't mind anything when he was getting ready for Neil. He'd trim his fingernails and toenails — it was a ritual for him, like he was preparing for some sacred ceremony.

"He writes all his own songs." My father was always reminding me that Neil Diamond was not just a great singer but also a songwriter. "Elvis never wrote a song. Hell, he never even played that guitar, that thing was just a prop." My father hated Elvis. Whenever Elvis came on the radio he'd turn it off or change the channel. "He didn't write that, you know." For some reason he saw Elvis as a threat, even though he had died back in the seventies. "Elvis got all the women, but Neil got all the talent." He said that all the time.

My father would always wear his best cowboy shirt. It was black with purple piping and he had a bolo tie to match. He'd put on his cowboy boots, and when he walked into the MGM Grand everybody would turn to look at him, especially the ladies. He'd act very nonchalant. Sometimes he'd say something to me, something pointless like, "What do you think of the decor?" He didn't give a shit about what I thought of the decor. Maybe I'd mutter, "It's cool," but he didn't care, and then we'd get our tickets for Neil Diamond. He'd have them reserved. The lady at the counter, Bernice, was a friend of his.

"Hello, Chester. Hi, Neil."

That was what my father named me — Neil. I hated my name. Sometimes I wondered what my mother would have called me, what my real name was.

"How are ya, darlin'?" my father would say.

"I'm doing good, baby."

Bernice was probably in her late forties. Her hair was colored orange and she wore so much hairspray and makeup that she looked like a wax figure. Sometimes people do things to make themselves look better and then they just keep going and they forget what their original intention was and by the time they're done they don't even look human anymore.

Bernice was always touching her hair, especially when she talked to my father. She'd be pretending to fix it but it wouldn't be moving, she'd just be sort of giggling and batting her lashes. They'd flirt for a little while and then she'd hand us the envelope with the tickets. Our names would be handwritten on the outside of the envelope along with some personal sentiment from her. One time she wrote:

Two tickets for Neil Diamond to the two cutest cutie-pies for miles around.

Love Berny

My father read this aloud, grinning. He'd had a brief fling with Bernice many years before. I don't know why he went to bed with her, but I'd always half suspected it from the way they flirted. One time I asked him and he said, "Oh yeah, long time ago I slipped her the old salami."

Bernice. She was one of those people who are *always* in a good mood. She was *always* "doing good, baby!" The first time you met her you'd think she was this terrifically friendly lady and then after seeing her a few times you'd begin to wonder what the hell was wrong with her. She was never sad or worried or upset. Just happy. All the time. It was like she was hiding something, like she was afraid of being found out. The veins tightened in her neck when she smiled. But then, that was everybody in Vegas, they all had that look, tight-faced, closed-off, clinging to their dirty secrets. Las Vegas was a city of poker faces. It was depressing seeing some guy from Ohio sitting in front of a slot machine at two in the morning with a beer in his hand and his wife tearfully pleading with him to come to bed and stop losing their money. One time I saw a man hit his wife in the face, like it was her fault that the sevens never came up.

My father would play a couple of hands of blackjack before we went to see the show. I wasn't allowed to play. You had to be twenty-one. I'd watch my father play his hands, drink his Midori, and chat with the dealer. He knew a lot of the dealers. He'd chat with them about how stupid the tourists were as the dealer kept taking his money. My father wouldn't even blink as the dealer swiped the twenty-five-dollar chips off his square and put them back in the slot where they'd been just a minute earlier.

He'd play a few hands and then he'd pocket his chips and we'd head to the Hollywood Theater. This was when my father always seemed to go into a trance. I knew better than to say anything because he wouldn't hear it. He'd move toward the doors of the Hollywood Theater like he was drawn by some magnetic force. He'd start walking differently, his hips loosened, his shoulders relaxed, his mouth dropped open. He'd hold out his ticket to be torn and just stare straight ahead. It was like he couldn't wait to get that first glimpse of the stage.

"He added a backup singer," he'd say to himself. Sure enough, there was an extra microphone stand for a third backup singer.

The funny thing is, my father wasn't the only one. There were other men with that faraway look in their eyes — they came alone or they came with dates, but either way they were unmistakable. They reminded me of all those stray dogs in the desert, lost and alone, half dead from the heat. They reminded me of all the dogs that lived at the ends of chains on the burnt backyard lawns of the locals, the life drained out of them, their heavy coats soaking up the blazing sun, dogs that were never meant to be near a desert. That was what they looked like to me, these men, with their mouths turned down, the hard lines carved across their foreheads. Dogs. Frightened and dizzy from a lifetime of bad luck, their choke collars strangling their throats, held firmly on invisible leashes, held firmly by ghosts from their past. But here was where they felt safe. Here was where Neil Diamond took them away from themselves and told them that everything was going to be OK. When I watched these men sitting on their soft chairs in the dark, I saw their faces change — his music gave them hope. Their eyes became bright, and for those brief ninety minutes Neil Diamond set them free.

4

I T WAS LATE. All the lights were off. When my father was up he'd usually sit in the living room with the lights off and the TV on, flipping the channels, searching for comedians.

"Oh my God, can you believe he's talking about that?" my father would exclaim while listening to a comedian do a routine about lying in bed with a new lover and having to pass gas. My father would be going, "Oh no, oh my God!" He couldn't get enough of comedy on those cable shows. Sometimes, in the morning, he'd tell one of the routines to Kimmy and me at breakfast and he'd screw it up. He'd leave out some important piece of information so the joke wouldn't make any sense. I'd usually pretend to laugh so that it didn't get too awkward, but sometimes I wouldn't. If he'd been rough with me the night before I might just sit there. Sometimes he'd start to explain it and Kimmy would just light another cigarette, suck on it for a while and tell him, "Yeah, we get it, it's just not funny when you do it."

"I'm doing it like the guy on TV."

She'd say, "No, when he did it, it was funny."

And then my father would look at me but by then I would be pretending to be fascinated by something in my cereal.

I popped the trunk. I grabbed the shovel that my father kept in the corner of the garage. We lived on about forty acres and my father was always digging up fence posts and replacing them. He was very diligent about keeping the land in order — it was the house that was never finished. He'd been putting an addition on the back of the house for three years now. He'd torn the exterior wall down, roughed it in, and then covered it with a plastic sheet because he was going on a trip with some lady that he'd met at the Luxor Hotel. She'd never seen Neil Diamond in concert, so my father found out where he was playing and they flew off to Cleveland for three days. When he came back he was so embroiled in the new romance that he never got around to putting a wall up, and so for three years we'd had no back wall on our house, just this big sheet of clear plastic stapled to the two-by-fours. In the morning the sun would come blasting through and you'd have to squint just to see your breakfast. After a while, sand had begun blowing into the house through small tears in the sheet, and my father had had to rip it down and put up a new one. That plastic could really make a racket. When a storm blew up, it sounded like one of the jets from the Air Force base was flying straight into the house.

I dropped the shovel into the trunk beside Blackie and then grabbed the trunk lid and closed it as quietly as I could.

"Where the hell have you been?"

I looked into my father's eyes. He was standing in the garage, facing me with a drink in his hand.

"I was at Fred's house."

"I know where you were," he said. He was looking at his watch. "What time did you say you were going to be home?"

"Midnight."

"And what time is it?"

"One."

The bump over his right eye was bright red. He was standing a few inches from my face. "You've been drinking." It wasn't a question.

"I had a couple of beers."

He grabbed me by the back of the neck and pushed my face down on the trunk. "And you drove my car? You got a fucking pea-sized brain if you think that's OK."

He had my left arm around my back and was twisting it. It was a police hold that he had learned at the academy. I'd seen him use it once when he broke up a fight between a couple of winos outside the movie theater downtown.

When I was in the fourth grade my father came to school and showed all the kids the different police holds, demonstrating how they could protect themselves from an attack. I could tell that he was as thrilled as the kids were. After the demonstration, he took us out to the parking lot and showed us how to operate his police radio. I remember that day so clearly. I remember how all the kids were in awe of my father and how they wished that their fathers could be just like mine. For the rest of the day I had to try and force myself to keep from grinning. See, I had something that none of the other kids had, I had something that made me the envy of the whole rest of the school. My father was sheriff of the city of Carmen.

"How do you think it would make me look if my boy got picked up for drunken driving?" I knew there was no answer I could give to make him loosen his grip, so I kept my mouth shut. "I'm talking to you!"

"I'm sorry."

"Sorry? Get inside!" He gave my arm a yank and I slingshotted into the house.

Kimmy was watching television. She didn't turn around when we walked into the dining room; she just kept watching TV. Her chair faced away from us so that all we could see was her elbow on the armrest and a cloud of smoke above the chair. There was a comedian on TV playing a guitar designed to look like a naked woman, and he wore a fireman's hat that doubled as a squirt gun. Between verses water shot out from his hat and soaked the crowd. It sounded like the crowd was roaring with laughter, but whenever the camera fixed on them they were just sitting there looking bored. Kimmy changed the channel, searching for something worth watching. She stopped at an *A&E Biography* on the JFK assassination. They were showing Jackie Kennedy standing stoically as the new president was sworn in.

"You didn't think about that, did you?" My father was talking about how I could have ruined his reputation if I'd been pulled over.

"No, sir, I guess I didn't."

"You guess you didn't? You *know* you didn't! You *know* you didn't!" He poured what was left of his Midori down his throat. "You think you're something special?"

"No, sir."

"You got that right."

Kimmy didn't move during all of this, just stared at the television. I don't know what I expected her to do; maybe I wanted her to take my side, maybe I wanted her to tell him to shut up and leave me alone.

"You got that right!" I could tell that he was pretty plowed because he was repeating himself. He smacked me in the head and my hat came off. "What's the rule about hats in the house? You want to play football?"

"Yeah."

"Huh?"

"Yes."

"'Cause I'll pull the cord. Is that what you want?"

"No."

"Huh? What am I going to do with you? I just . . . am I not getting through to you?" He looked to Kimmy for support but she didn't say a thing, she wasn't getting involved, her only response was a series of lazy smoke rings floating defiantly up from behind her chair.

"The both of ya," he muttered. "I'm trying to teach you responsibility. Responsibility!"

I nodded.

"What did I say?"

"You're teaching me responsibility."

"That's not what I —"

"You're *trying* to teach me responsibility."

"*I'm* trying to teach you. Am I speaking Portuguese?"

"No."

"What language am —"

"English."

"Oh, very good. Now let's try it. Pick up that apple from the table and put it over there on the counter."

"Pardon me?"

"Now!"

I took an apple from a bowl on the table and placed it gently on the counter.

"Was that difficult?"

"No."

"Was it painful?"

I shook my head.

"We're going to get a little more challenging now. Fetch Kimmy's cigarettes and toss them in the garbage."

"But . . ." I glanced over and saw Kimmy snatch her cigarettes off the side table.

"But . . . but . . . ," he repeated, mocking me.

The telephone rang in the kitchen. We both stopped and looked at it. Occasionally my father would get calls from the station late at night because the department was understaffed.

He picked up the receiver. I knew it was Quinlan down at the station, I could hear his high-pitched voice. Quinlan was one of my father's deputies. He was in his late twenties and had been a cop for only a few years. Even though he was a strapping guy, he sounded like a little boy; his voice was a thin, high-pitched squeak and it took some getting used to. My father didn't say a word. He just stood there and listened. All he said was "Done" and then he hung up.

He stood there scratching his temple, thinking to himself. "Some lady says her kid is missing . . . few miles down the road." He unwrapped a packet of gum and popped a couple of pieces into his mouth. He chewed them for a minute and stared at his feet. He was drunk. My father could appear sober even after he'd drunk a whole case. He could really put it away, just sit there sipping, the glass looking foolish in his giant hand, until the bottle was gone. And never once did I ever hear my father say that he'd had too much to drink. Not even when he woke up on the floor and had to step over broken furniture to get to the coffee.

"I want to see you drive."

"You want —"

"I want to see just what the hell you were doing out there."

We got into the car. He took my Nirvana CD out of the stereo and dropped it on the floor. He shoved in Neil Diamond's 1966 Bang record, *The Feel of Neil*, and didn't say another word.

5

I PULLED INTO the driveway and parked behind a cream-colored Lincoln Touring Sedan. The kid's family lived off the highway in a small enclave where it looked like some guy had considered building a subdivision, put up four houses, and then changed his mind. They'd moved in over the summer and still didn't have a lawn. It was just sand. The entire front of their house was bare.

Mrs. Curtis was the first one to greet us. She came running out of the house wearing a cardigan and stretch pants. Mr. Curtis and his daughter Mary followed behind her. Through their living-room window I could see they'd been watching the same A&E program as Kimmy.

"Are you the sheriff?" Mrs. Curtis was holding my father's arm.

"It's all right, ma'am, just calm down."

"We're new here," she said. "My son is missing."

"When did you see him last?"

"We just moved here in August."

"That's OK." My father had a way of calming people down. He was so large and imposing, standing there and casually chewing his gum, that you just knew that with him on your side everything was going to be OK.

"He went over to a friend's house for dinner. Kevin Bottoms. We called there. Kevin was home. He said that he'd said good-bye to Ian on the road over an hour ago. We never let him stay out this late. His bedtime is nine o'clock."

"Let me get my book," my father said.

He kept his report book in a briefcase in the trunk. He turned to me. "Go get my book, son. This is my son, Neil." I shook hands with Ian's father.

"Mom, he's fine," said Mary. Mary was embarrassed. She was rolling her eyes. I recognized her from school. She sat with a couple of other girls and watched our football practices.

They were all standing by the front of the car. I walked to the trunk with the keys in my hand. I felt sick; I wanted to vomit. I was hoping that I would open the trunk and he wouldn't be there anymore.

I pushed the key into the slot and glanced up to make sure that nobody else could see what I was about to see. I opened the trunk and stared at him lying in a broken heap. He'd shifted during the ride over and now he was staring straight up at me with his eyes and mouth wide open. I started looking around for my father's briefcase. I could hear Mrs. Curtis talking about what a good boy Ian was and how he never stayed out past his bedtime. Mr. Curtis didn't say a word, just stood quietly by his wife's side, letting her carry on. Mary kept jumping in with, "Mom, he's fine, you worry too much."

"Son, have you got the book?"

I couldn't find my father's briefcase. I was feeling around behind Ian's body for it, but there was nothing there.

"It's not back here." I knew what was coming next. I pushed Ian's body as far back as I could, back into the shadow, and closed the trunk as my father approached.

"Give me the keys." He took the keys from me.

"It's not there."

I stood away from the car. I had nowhere to go but toward the family. I walked toward Mrs. Curtis. She was smiling at me. I stood with them and for a second I felt safe, as if they might protect me. I looked into Mrs. Curtis's eyes and I could see how scared she was, see how much she loved her son, and for a crazy second I thought that maybe I could replace him.

The sound of the key going into the slot was sharp and cold. I held my breath as the trunk opened and I waited for my father to give me away. Mrs. Curtis sounded a million miles away, like she was on a distant planet and I was watching it all on a satellite. She wouldn't stop talking about her son. Part of me just wanted to scream, "He's dead! Your son is dead and it was an accident!" But I didn't. I kept quiet and pretended to listen as she told us about how carefully Ian rode his bicycle. I don't know why she was talking about her kid's riding a bicycle. I guess she was proud of him. Or maybe she was remembering him. Maybe a part of her already knew he was gone and she was replaying the happy moments out loud so that we could hear about what it must be like to still be innocent.

And then I heard the trunk slam shut. My father came back with the book. He took down a description of Ian from Mrs. Curtis — five-three, ninety-six pounds, black hair, with a scar on his forehead from when he'd fallen off his bike. It sounded like she was describing a corpse, like she already knew he was dead.

My father didn't look at me, he just wrote down the information. While he wrote, I noticed Mary watching me. She kept smiling and twisting her ankle like she was doing a stretching exercise.

"Hi." That was all she said. I tried to smile but I couldn't, I just sort of nodded my head.

Mrs. Curtis wanted to know what my father was going to do. He told her that he couldn't file a report until the morning and hopefully Ian would turn up before then. And then she turned to her husband and said, "Maybe I should call Clive." My father stopped writing and looked up.

Mr. Curtis spoke. "Her brother Clive. He's FBI in Philadelphia."

My father nodded. He hated FBI agents. He called them accountants with guns. "I don't think that's necessary," he said.

The last thing I remember before we got into the car and drove home was Mrs. Curtis's laugh. It was deep and full and sounded strange coming from a person who was so scared. My father said something about the spanking Ian was going to get when he got home. Maybe she was just relieved to hear that somebody thought her son was going to be OK. He made a joke about how children didn't realize how difficult it was to be a parent, but not to worry because it would be their turn soon enough. All of the Curtises had a good chuckle at that.

On the way back my father drove and I sat in the passenger seat. He didn't turn on the stereo. We drove in silence. He removed a silver flask from his jacket and took a couple of belts.

We pulled into the garage and got out of the car. I went upstairs. I sat on my bed and waited. I waited to hear him go to sleep. I waited to see the lights go off downstairs and for the silence to tell me that it was safe. Every couple of minutes I peeked around the corner. His bedroom was downstairs across from the kitchen. He didn't like walking up and down the stairs with his bad knee. He'd blown his right knee out playing ball for Oklahoma State and now he walked with a slight limp although he disguised it so that some people thought he just had his own style of motion. Although my father was in his fifties, he didn't look it. He looked closer to forty. He was still in really good shape.

I heard footsteps coming up the stairs. I turned out the lights and got into bed. My father knocked on the door and before I could tell him to come in, he did.

"How's the team this year?"

"It's okay." My throat was dry but I was afraid to swallow

because I didn't want him to know that I was scared. His eyes were in shadow — all I could see was the outline of his head from the light in the hallway.

He just stood there and finally he walked out and closed the door. I lay in my bed staring at the ceiling, listening to him walk back down the stairs. I lay there playing it over in my head, feeling the thud as Ian bounced off the front of my father's car. I thought that maybe if I played it over enough times in my head I could convince myself that it had just been a dream. After a while, I turned my bedside light on and stared at the photograph of my mother.

6

WHEN I LOOKED at the photograph of my mother, I felt like I was staring at a stranger. Sometimes I tried to remember that moment. The moment that the shutter of the camera opened and caught this happy family. But I couldn't.

I could remember other things about that time. I remember my father handing me a Sno-Kone. I remember him lifting me up on his shoulders while I stared down at the ground. I felt safe up there with my hands holding tightly on to his forehead. I couldn't believe I'd ever felt safe with my father, but that was what I remembered.

When I thought about my mother, it was a blank. Except for that moment in the laundry room, I couldn't remember a thing. Sometimes I'd sit in class and try to force myself to remember. I'd create these images and then I'd wonder if they were true. I'd imagine walking down the street holding her hand or riding next to her in the car — things that must have happened — but nothing came back. I'd try to imagine her buying me candy or taking me to get my hair cut, but it was useless.

Sometimes I'd watch television, looking for her. I thought that maybe I might see her on a commercial selling laundry detergent or breakfast cereal. In the summer, I'd watch the soap operas, looking for her. I guessed that she'd moved to Los Angeles and married some dentist and probably never spoke about the family that she'd left back in Carmen. I imagined that she probably had a bunch of kids now and lived in a mansion in Beverly Hills.

She'd been eighteen when she married my father, and he'd been twice her age. She'd gotten pregnant and so they'd gotten married. She must have hated it out here in the middle of nowhere. She'd had to quit her job at the Sands, all because my father had knocked her up.

My father never talked to me about my mother. I knew that she had run away from her home — that's what my father's deputy Ronald Stokely told me once. He didn't know the details, but she'd come from a bad family and she'd run away. She'd run to Vegas and met my father and then all of a sudden I'd come along. I imagined how my father must have treated her, the fights they must have had. She'd probably wanted to go out and have fun but she couldn't because of me. She was young, she was in a situation that she hated, and so she split. We were a bad family and so she just kept running. I tossed this around all the time, imagining what had happened, imagining what he must have done to make her leave. It kept me up at night. I'd lie there toss-ing and turning, getting more agitated, trying to untangle this mystery.

My report cards were always saying, "Neil doesn't listen in class." It was true. I focused all my energy on trying to figure out *why?* I needed to know *why* she'd left. I needed to know *why* she hadn't taken me with her and *why* we looked so happy in that photograph. I just couldn't concen-trate on anything until I answered all the endless *why*s.

I stared at the clock, wondering when my father was go-ing to go to bed. He had one of those CD changers where he could line up five CDs at once. He just sat down there play-ing one Neil Diamond record after another. He listened to *Headed for the Future* and then *Hot August Night, Beauti-ful Noise, The Jazz Singer,* and finally *Tap Root Manuscript.*

At 6:18 A.M. I heard the shower go on downstairs.

My father liked to get up early. Kimmy didn't get up un-til eight-thirty — she'd sleep in as long as possible and then rush around trying to get ready for work. I'd usually get to school on the bus, except during football season. Dur-ing football season my father drove me in to school early.

When I heard the shower go on, I went downstairs, tip-toed past my father's bedroom, and went out to the garage. I didn't know what I was going to do with the body, I just knew that I had to get it out of the trunk. I had to get rid of it.

My heart was pounding. I was terrified that my father might open the door or somebody else might appear. I could feel my heart slamming against my chest. I didn't want to see him. Ian. He had a name now. His mother must have said his name twenty times. I couldn't get his mother out of my mind, standing there, grabbing onto my father's arm, pleading with him to help her.

I sat in the driver's seat and popped the trunk. I was scared to look at his body, scared of what he might look like in the daylight, scared that seeing the body might make things even more real. I walked around to the back of the car and looked into the trunk.

And it was empty.

I gasped. And then, for a moment, I felt relief. Total relief. I checked the back of the trunk. Nothing. The body was gone. I breathed in the warm desert air. I don't know why, maybe because I wanted it so badly, but for a second I thought that it had been a dream — that it had all been just some sort of drunken dream. There *was* no body. There had never been a body. I wanted to laugh. I wanted to scream. Yes, I had lost my mind, just gone crazy for a moment, and now everything was OK. I wanted to jump up and down and hug total strangers, but I couldn't. I couldn't because I knew it wasn't true.

I staggered out of the garage. I collapsed on the gravel and I began to puke. I puked until my stomach was empty — I wanted to keep going until there was nothing left of me, until all of the sickness I felt inside of me was gone. I knelt there on my hands and knees, holding on to the sharp gravel, and I began to hear Neil Diamond. I could hear him singing. It just kept going through my head and I couldn't shut it off. The Earth was spinning out of control and I couldn't move and all I could hear was Neil Diamond screaming his song into my ear.

The sun was coming up. It was going to be another perfect, hot day in the desert. The sky was going to be a deep, cloudless blue, there was going to be a warm, gentle breeze, and everything was going to be exactly the same as it had been yesterday. People were getting up and putting on their clothes and washing their hair and eating their eggs and reading their newspapers. And my father was in the shower, washing himself clean.

MONDAY

7

I WENT BACK up the stairs and into my bathroom. I heard my father turn off the shower. I couldn't believe that he'd just gone into the shower a few minutes ago; it seemed like years had gone by.

I took a shower and put on my clothes. I went downstairs. My father was sitting at the table, eating a bowl of corn-flakes. He didn't speak, just pushed the milk toward me after I filled my bowl with cereal. I glanced at him but he was staring into his bowl and shoveling cereal into his mouth. I tried to see if he looked tired but I could never tell with him, he was so handsome that he never looked tired, even after a full night of binge drinking.

He drove me to school. I had football practice at seven-thirty. He popped in Neil Diamond's '67 record *Just for You* and began humming along.

My father had a beautiful singing voice. Even when he

hummed it was deep and resonant and always in perfect pitch. I remember when I was a kid and he sang in church, I always felt embarrassed that he sang so loud. I think if he hadn't become a cop, he probably would have been a lounge act. His voice was that good. I think my father went to church to live out his fantasy of being Neil Diamond. When he sang I could hear a little bit of Neil, like my father was winking at him and saying, "I know these people think I'm here to worship Jesus, but we both know who's really the King of the Jews."

I'd heard from Stokely that my father had become very depressed the day he found out that Neil Diamond was Jewish. It was back in the early eighties. They'd gone to see Neil Diamond in *The Jazz Singer* and my father had walked out in a daze. I think my father was just surprised. I guess it was understandable; I mean, Neil Diamond did put out a Christmas album. Anyway, my father didn't eat for a week, he was forgetful and preoccupied, and then one day he showed up at work wearing a Star of David around his neck. After that he wouldn't tolerate anyone's saying anything derogatory with regard to the Jewish faith. He even looked into the possibility of converting. One Sunday afternoon he drove into Vegas to talk to a rabbi. He came back looking shaken. The rabbi had told him that there was a lot of work you had to do before they let you become Jewish. My father said there was just way too much "rigmarole." And so we stayed Protestant. If you were Protestant all you had to do was show up. And really you didn't even have to do that.

I stared out the car window. We didn't speak. I didn't

know what to say. I was hung over, I hadn't slept, but I'd never felt more wide-awake in my life. I could feel my pulse thumping in my neck.

We passed the spot on the highway where I had killed Ian. I could see the skid marks where I'd slammed on my brakes after hitting him and the deep gouges in the gravel where I'd peeled away. I don't know why, but for some reason I played it over in my head. I don't know if I did it to torture myself or in the hope of making it turn out differently. I imagined that I saw his face. He was running, terrified, watching me, trying to get out of the way. I swung the wheel to the right and instinctively slammed my foot down hard on the floor, and then I realized where I was. My father just kept driving, looking straight ahead, not saying a word.

We were driving through downtown Carmen. My hometown. It was drab and brown and just sort of melted into the desert. The sand got onto everything and nothing stayed clean for very long. If you painted your shutters white they were turning brown by the end of the week. Even the people seemed brown, just tired and worn out. There were slot machines everywhere in Carmen, in convenience stores, gas stations, and supermarkets, but nobody ever won. Seeing old ladies with their grocery carts full of cat food while stuffing quarters into the slot machines just about made me want to tear my eyes out.

My father made a left instead of a right, heading away from the school. He pulled into the Chevron station. I noticed that he had two thirds of a tank left. I wanted to ask him why he was going to the gas station. I wanted to ask him what he'd done with Ian Curtis's body. I wanted to ask him what was behind that faraway look in his eye.

As he drove toward the sign that read CARWASH, I realized what he was doing. He was getting rid of the evidence. He paid the attendant six dollars, and I was waiting for him to say something like, "You should be paying for this one," but he didn't. My father was cheap. When he first started going out with Kimmy he hired a skywriter for her birthday. This guy wrote out little messages in the sky with the pollution from his airplane. My father wanted the message to read "CHESTER LOVES KIMMY." When he found out that the guy charged by the letter, he got him to write C ♥ K. That was it. He got it down to three letters. And when she saw it she cried, she said it was the most beautiful thing she'd ever seen.

He put the car into neutral and the machine dragged us into the building. I'd loved car washes when I was a kid. The foamy water spraying against the window, obstructing my view, and me, in the backseat, dry and safe, while the machines worked in perfect harmony. That morning, I just felt trapped. I didn't want my view obstructed. I was afraid to be alone in the car with my father.

He was nodding his head slowly to the music and watching as the hose shot torpedoes of water at the car. Whatever sins may have been attached to the front grille of my father's Eldorado were washed away and disappeared down a drain at seven o'clock that October morning.

8

TEMPO, TEMPO, TEMPO, TEMPO!" Coach Ulster was in a bad mood. "Ahhh, goddamn it, you made me drop my gum!"

We were playing Las Vegas High School on Saturday, they were ranked number one in the state. We were number two and Ulster was aching for a win. He always took it hard when we lost. The previous year, when LVHS had beaten us for the pennant, Ulster had cried. It was embarrassing coming off the field and seeing him bawling his eyes out.

As my father pulled up to the school I felt this wave of fear. I wasn't looking forward to facing all the guys who had seen the way I'd behaved the night before. We were early. My father always got me to practice early. He said that if you were going to be a leader then you needed to be willing to do what no one else would do. The only other person at the school was Joe Maine, our waterboy. He was struggling across the parking lot with a jug of water in one hand and a bucket full of orange wedges in the other. He nodded at me and I waved back. I liked Joe. He was the size of a peanut but he wanted to play football and so Ulster let him warm up with the team in return for getting up at five-thirty every morning to slice oranges and carry the water to the field.

Carmen High was a big football school. There were only six hundred people in the entire student body, so even to be ranked was a major feat. The faculty claimed not to favor the athletes but they did, we were always handing in assignments late and not getting docked. The teachers had an understanding with Ulster, who aside from being coach also happened to be our principal. As long as you showed up for practice and gave 110 percent you could pretty much just float. He'd raise shit occasionally when one of the guys pushed the envelope, but when it came down to it, if you were on the starting lineup you were going to get the grades you needed.

We really took advantage of some of the teachers, especially Mr. Russell. Russell taught algebra. He was a hunched-over, wobbly kind of guy who wore the same blue, threadbare polyester pants every day and reeked of body odor. He loved math. He'd get very excited when he was teaching, dancing around on his toes while he worked out a problem on the board. He had no idea how silly he looked. I don't know, maybe he didn't care. He'd start to talk faster and his voice would go up a register.

We'd throw chalk at him when he wasn't looking and yell in class while he was writing on the board. And when he turned around we'd pretend to be studying. We'd just be yelling nonsense, like "Whoop!" or "Aaah!" And we'd really yell, I mean we would scream. It was a competition to see who could scream the loudest. We did it to torment him. He'd start to shake, just stand there trembling like a wet dog, helpless, with the chalk in his hand. Sometimes we'd blame one of the other kids. One time Russell laid into this effeminate boy named Steven Milne, just went nuts on him. We were all biting our hands to keep from laughing.

"Farby, you pussy, bend those knees, let's go now!"

Ulster had us all lined up and one after another we were running full tilt into the blocking sled.

"C'mon, let's move it, you little pussy farts! I want to see some damage now, let's go!" He was standing on the sidelines with a giant bag of sunflower seeds in his hand. He was addicted to them, leaving little piles of seeds up and down the sidelines with birds hovering over him like he was the saint of all creation. He'd be yelling at us and there'd be seeds on his teeth and this dry paste all over his lips and cheeks and the last thing anybody wanted was to follow orders from some clown with no table manners.

I ran against the sled and felt like I was going to vomit again.

"Garvin!"

"Yessir?"

"You're hitting that thing like it's the last piece of pussy on Earth. Bend those knees and put some heart into it."

I hated Ulster. He would tell us that we were all just

parts in a machine, a very simple, eleven-man machine. "Let's not try and complicate things by getting personalities," he would say. And he lied to us. His pep talks were filled with war stories from his past that were supposed to inspire us, but they were so obviously double-barreled cowshit that it shocked me when I looked around the room and saw that everyone else was lapping them up.

"How you feelin'?" Reed was behind me.

"Been better."

"You were pretty fucked up last night." Reed had a way of making his voice go up at the end of a sentence and turning a statement into a question so that unless you responded, it just sat in the air making you feel awkward.

"Yeah," I replied.

"Some of the guys are pretty pissed at you, especially Fred. What you said about Amy." I could feel his breath on my neck. "This is our year, bro . . . this is do or die." He was whispering to me because Stubby Fluke was standing in front of us. Stubby was our other receiver. Stubby hated both of us. At the party after the southern state championship the previous year, Stubby had accused me of favoring Reed with the ball. He was furious because college scouts from all over the Southwest had been at the game and he hadn't scored any points. We took it outside and they had to pull us off each other.

The thing is, Stubby was right, even Ulster had accused me of it — I did favor Reed with the ball. Since the morning that he first arrived from Bakersfield I'd been throwing the ball to him every day in the backyard of his house. We used to practice the same play over and over again. It was simple: Reed would go deep and I'd fade back until he was crossing the end zone and then I'd let it go and when we timed it perfectly he'd glance over his right shoulder just as the ball floated into his arms. We practiced that play thousands of times in Reed's backyard, over and over again until it invaded us nightly in our dreams. We used to play until it got dark; I'd just keep throwing the ball until he couldn't see it anymore, until it started landing in his face. And Reed never complained — he never had a problem playing hurt. I'd throw the ball and it would disappear into the fading light and then I'd hear "Ugh" and know that I'd given him another bloody nose and that it was time to go home.

After the fight with Stubby, Reed had driven me home. It had been an incredible day, with Reed catching all my throws, and after the game scouts from all over introducing themselves. That night we sat in Reed's car talking about our future. Our future, like it was one, and I remember Reed's saying how great it would be if we ended up playing for the same college. And I agreed. It was sort of like a pact.

Stubby took the game more seriously than the rest of us. It was no secret that Stubby wanted one thing out of high school: a football scholarship from a major college. He didn't sit with the team at lunch, he sat with his girlfriend, Stacey — his protein powders and vitamins spread out on the table in front of him. He was an amateur nutritionist, Stubby was, and he kept records on everything.

Stubby's father would sit on the bleachers, chewing his gum and watching the field. He was just like his son, barely talking to the other fathers. Occasionally he'd pull a pad out of his shirt pocket and scribble down notes to discuss with Stubby at dinner that evening.

A lot of the fathers would come to the practices. They were mostly blue-collar guys who punched a clock in Vegas and resided in Carmen, where you got *more home for your buck*. They held down the kind of jobs that advertised ON-THE-JOB-TRAINING — temporary positions that dragged on forever. Fred's father was a card dealer and so was Farby's. The Penguin's father worked security at Ballys, and Benny Jericho's old man played guitar nightly for some singer in the lounge of the Continental Hotel. In the mornings they would drive their sons to practice and hang out on the bleachers, joshing each other and spilling coffee on themselves. All of them were divorced, some on their second, third, or fourth marriages, and most of them had that look in their eyes that I'd seen in the men waiting for Neil Diamond — they'd walked away from their dreams and they were just killing time. They would even joke about it, about the *crazy dreams* of their youth. It bothered me; it seemed like a taunt, a way of telling us, their sons, that we were foolish, that it wasn't going to work out for us either. But at the same time these men would shell out money they didn't have to equip their sons with the most updated gear and they'd show up at every practice to cheer them on. It was confusing. They wanted their sons to succeed yet they'd tell them not to get their hopes up. But all we had was hope. That was all we had. I guess deep down they didn't believe in their sons because after all, their sons had come from them.

Getting recruited was the secret dream of every one of the players. It wasn't something that most of us talked about, but you felt it every time a scout showed up at a game. The whispers would ripple through the bench and leap out into the field, spreading through the offensive line until everybody was playing at a different level.

"OK, let's go, Garvin!"

I crouched down and stared at the blocking sled. That was when I noticed that one of the guys holding it was Fred. He was staring back at me with this sad look in his eyes. Big, slow, sweet-faced Fred. I used to snicker to myself whenever I thought about him. He was dim. If he weren't on the football team, there was no way he'd be getting passing grades. Most of the girls giggled when he walked past; he was like some grotesque bear, a borderline case. But there was something in him that I'd never noticed before. He was happy. He had his football and Amy and his double lunches, his father was his best friend, and he loved his mother with complete devotion. His mother made these extravagant lunches for Fred that we used to tease him about until we realized that it didn't bother him. She prepared these gourmet sandwiches that went on forever — olives and peppers and ham and onions and homemade breads — these works of art that Fred gobbled down like an angry ape. Most of the kids ate peanut-butter sandwiches or their parents threw them a few bucks and they ate the slop from the cafeteria; the only purpose of lunch was to curb your hunger until you got home and your mother made you a proper meal. I think that was why Fred's lunches caused such envy: his mother was with him even when he was with his friends.

"Garvin, let's move it!" Ulster was getting edgy.

I stared at Fred and he stared back at me. He didn't look angry. It would have been easier if he did. He looked hurt. I could feel all of the energy seeping out of me and I realized that I couldn't have made it to the sled even if I'd wanted to. I looked over at Ulster and I pulled my helmet off. "I'm not feeling too good today, Coach."

"I don't give a poodle crap how you're feeling, Garvin. You hit that goddamn sled with some serious g-force or you hit the showers and don't ever think about setting foot on my field again!"

I hated Ulster. I hated the way he pushed us, the way he just didn't give a shit about anybody. I really hated him. Hated his guts. I mean, I just hated him.

"I don't feel like it, Coach." I don't know where it came from, but I just didn't care. Ulster had this expression like he couldn't believe what I was saying.

"You little pussy fart, I want you to hit that fucking sled right now. Right now!" I'd never heard Ulster use the word *fuck* before. He was always calling us pussy farts, but he never actually swore. It jolted me. I actually turned and looked at the sled. I was about to run at it until I caught another glance at Fred. I wanted Fred to nod at me, to somehow give me permission, tell me it was OK, but he didn't.

"Move it! Now! Now!" All my teammates were staring at me. I hesitated. Ulster was losing his authority with every passing second. "You walk off this field, Garvin, and that's it, don't even think of coming back!" He looked like a fish. He had jowls. I guess some people can age overnight. I never remembered seeing his jowls before, but now they were trembling. They made him look weak and harmless. "You're throwing away your future, you know that."

My future. I just sort of mumbled, "I can't." I walked through the team with my head down and shuffled off the field.

9

"WHAT ARE YOU DOING?" Reed ran up beside me.

"Leave me alone."

"I can't believe you." That was what he said. And he was right. "Just 'cause you don't like him . . . Jesus! I don't understand what you're doing."

Some of the school buses had started to arrive in the parking lot, and there were already a few students sitting in the bleachers along with some of the players' fathers. I noticed Mary Curtis sitting beside Julie Sorge — Julie was in my algebra class, her clothes were dirty and discount, she was nice, but nobody paid much attention to her. And there was Lenore, standing by herself at the top of the hill. She looked heartbroken, like she'd been crying all night.

I didn't know if I loved Lenore, I didn't know how I felt. I think I wanted to love her. One time she told me that she loved me and so I told her the same and then we never talked about it again. I was always managing to say the wrong thing, but for some reason she made me feel like everything I hated about myself didn't matter. And it wasn't like she tried to convince me. Girls will do that. One time I messed around with Kate Urmswood and she kept telling me that I was a *beautiful person*. It made me want to move to a forest and live off of bark. I knew that she was just trying to convince herself. I didn't argue with her but I sure wasn't horny anymore. I guess more than anyone Lenore accepted whatever it was about me that I couldn't, and that's why she was my girlfriend. I don't know why I was her boyfriend. I wondered about that all the time.

She watched me walk across the field toward her. I caught her eye and then she turned around and started walking away. She walked through the parking lot and into the school.

I could hear some of the students talking about me.

"What are we going to do about a quarterback?"

"They'll get somebody else. He was an asshole anyway."

I could feel my stomach flipping open like a trap door. I remembered hearing my English teacher, Mrs. Aemes, use the term "persona non grata." She was talking about some guy who had snitched on the Mob, some movie she'd seen from the forties. This guy was despised by everybody — his friends, his family — and finally even his wife left him. He had to leave the town forever and he questioned whether he had done the right thing. If he'd stayed and kept his mouth shut his life could have gone on the same as before.

But I just couldn't run up against that sled, no matter what Ulster called me. He could have called me a pussy fart for the rest of the day, I just couldn't run into that sled with Fred Billings staring back at me.

I'd called his girlfriend a Cyclops.

He probably even wanted to forgive me. He probably wanted to explain it away, just like people had done with me for most of my life. Lately they'd made excuses for me because I had what the local paper called a *Million-Dollar Arm*. As long as I was winning games for Carmen a lot of people just put up with my behavior, labeling it *rambunctious*, but as I walked toward the locker room I realized that I was about to become persona non grata.

In the first game of the season I'd thrown a pass fifty-four yards to Reed for a touchdown. Carl Elders wrote a story on me for the *Monitor.* They showed the pass on ESPN's Clips of the Week. It was big news. After that there were scouts coming out to all of our games and even to some of our practices. Elders's half-page article went into detail about how some people have an extraordinary ability for no particular reason. He'd done research on it. He interviewed me to find out how I was able to throw so far with so much accuracy. I told him that I'd thrown the ball around a lot with my father since I was a little kid. But that was only part of it. The truth was that I masturbated excessively. My left arm was twice as strong as my right. What they called my great snap was due in large part to the fast-twitch muscles in my left wrist and forearm, developed through hundreds of hours spent perfecting my bomb in the upstairs bathroom of my father's house.

There was a scout from UNLV who had started coming to some of our practices. He first showed up the day after they televised the clip on television. His name was Norman Lime and he didn't look anything like what you'd expect from a scout. He was shaped like a swag lamp and had no hair on his head except for two tufts on either side that made him look like a clown — and every time I saw him he had a boil on his face, but it was always in a different place. One time it was on his lip and I couldn't even look at him, I just had to stare at my feet. It's not that I'm prejudiced against blemishes, I just think it's common courtesy for a person to acknowledge their boils, otherwise everyone they talk to ends up staring at the ground. Anyway, he'd started showing up again this season and a couple of weeks earlier he had let me and Reed drive his silver BMW around after our practice. He told us what great cars those BMWs were and how they liked to give them away as incentives to "promising athletes" to come and play for the college. He made it sound like everybody got one. I could tell that Reed was excited even though the next day he told me that he would never drive an import. So Lime dropped Reed off back in the parking lot and then he drove me home. On the way he asked me what I thought of Stubby Fluke. I froze. I wanted to tell him about Reed but I didn't, I said that Stubby was a real good player and a real hard worker. My face was burning. I felt guilty, like I was supposed to stand up for Reed. I wanted to, I wanted to explain what a great player Reed was, that he was dependable. I wanted to explain that we had a pact. Stubby was faster than Reed, but Reed had heart. Reed was the kind of player that you couldn't evaluate based on statistics — Reed would play hurt. It made me angry to even try to compare the two of them; I knew that I'd choose Reed over Stubby any day of the week. Stubby would never play hurt.

My father invited Lime in and treated the clown like he was royalty, gave him a glass of Midori on ice and told him this endless stream of dirty jokes that weren't funny but had Lime breathless with laughter. Lime told my father that he was very impressed with my arm. He called it *that arm,* like it was something I kept in my closet. He told my father that he would be keeping a close eye on me, and then they just winked at each other like a pair of quivering fruits. Later we walked Lime out to his car and he opened his trunk and presented me with a leather UNLV football jacket. I didn't tell Reed about the jacket. I didn't know how to tell him. Lime made me try the jacket on to see if it fit. It did.

Reed eventually found out about the jacket, though he never mentioned it. My father had told a couple of the other fathers and then it just got around. I felt ashamed that I hadn't stood up for him but I also felt angry that I'd had to make the decision. I couldn't stop wondering what he would have done in my position. The odds of two players' getting recruited by the same college were long, and it just wasn't the kind of thing that you could ask for. Reed's silence about the jacket made me angry. It was as if he was saying that he would have said something to Lime. And so for the past few weeks whenever I was around Reed I'd felt clammy.

There was a tap on my shoulder. It was Mary Curtis. She was wearing a pleated skirt and a thin cotton T-shirt that had a tiny little bow tie at the throat.

"Hi."

"Hi."

"Are you OK?" She was asking *me* if I was OK.

"Yeah."

"Thanks for coming by last night. My parents are freaking out. My brother hasn't come home yet. Nobody knows where he is." I didn't know what to say. I didn't know where her brother was either. "That looked pretty heavy out there."

"Yeah." We were walking down the hall. I saw Lenore at the end of the hall talking to Mr. Erickson, the music teacher. Lenore played the saxophone in the Carmen Stage Band. She saw me talking to Mary and then she turned and looked away.

"I better go take a shower," I said to Mary.

"OK, I'll see you later."

The locker room was empty. I sat on the bench and I listened to myself breathe. The stench of stale sweat normally bothered me and I didn't like to spend a lot of time in there but that morning I sort of enjoyed it. It felt familiar. There were guys on the team who would come in from a workout, take off their uniforms, put on their clothes, and go straight to class. They wouldn't take a shower. I wondered if they knew they stank. Maybe they didn't make the connection between sweating and stinking. Maybe they thought they were still children. Kids could run around all day and not smell, but once you hit puberty, bathing was supposed to be a daily habit. I guess some guys just hadn't figured it out yet. I wanted to tell them but it wasn't something that anybody ever talked about. Sometimes I wondered if anybody else even noticed.

I had my face in my hands and was making loud honking noises. I was trying to force myself to bawl but no tears were coming. It was embarrassing when I looked up and saw someone else in the room, this ninth-grader who ran on the cross-country team. He was this tall bony kid who ran to school every morning with his knapsack on his back. He kept glancing at me while he was getting undressed. Normally I'd have told somebody like that to go to hell but I just didn't feel like it now.

I took off my uniform and went into the showers, standing there with this kid a few feet away. It felt awkward being naked in the showers with this guy after he'd just seen me embarrass myself. I turned away from him and washed myself as quickly as I could.

I got dressed and walked down the hall to the cafeteria. There were a few students sitting around drinking sodas and shooting baskets into the trash with these hard little lunch apples that the school provided free of charge. Mr. Russell sat in the corner tutoring some students. I remembered that I had a math test that day. For a split second I felt panicked about the test and then it passed and I didn't feel anything.

10

I SAT IN HOMEROOM, pretending to go over my math notes. I could hear the whispers. It'd already spread through the school that I'd quit the football team.

At the back of the room, I could hear two guys making noises like we did in Russell's class.

"Whoop!"

"Ahhhh!"

It was Clyde and Dayton, cousins, ropy little trailer-park goons with bleeding gums and white greasy hair who always reeked of weed — the type of guys you'd expect to shoot up a school. They frequently wore these filthy homemade T-shirts with slogans like EAT MY ASS! They hated my guts for once humiliating them in front of some girls. I had said that they were descended from a long line of cousin-fuckers and that their gene pool had no deep end. I'd heard it from my father, who'd seen some comedian say it on *An Evening at the Improv*. I think it hurt their feelings and I wondered if I'd hit a nerve; they'd just packed up their books and skulked down the hall muttering to themselves in some strange white-trash dialect.

And now they were mocking me. The noises were directed at me and there was nothing I could do about it.

"Ahhhh!"

A couple of guys from the team were there, Benny Jericho and Ernie Gates. They sat in front of me and stared straight ahead. I was all alone. I buried my nose deeper into my notebook.

"Whoop!" "Aaaah!" They were making me look like a fool. Some of the other students were laughing. I wanted to get up and slam their heads together.

And then I heard, "Quitter." It was Dayton. His voice had gone terminally dopey from smoking so much weed. I turned around and stared at him. I tried to give him the dangerous look that my father threw me when he wanted to scare me.

They both went, "Ooooh." I turned back and faced the front of the room. There was nothing I could do. I could feel my back getting hot. My head was filling up with rage and confusion. They had won. They weren't afraid of me anymore and I'd lost face in front of everybody.

Mrs. Aemes walked into the classroom. She'd been out in the hall getting the stragglers to hurry up.

The bell went off and everybody stood up for the national anthem. I could hear Clyde and Dayton giggling at the back of the room.

During the anthem, a spitball hit me in the back of the head.

11

ABOUT THREE HUNDRED students from Carmen High School along with a couple of Nevada highway patrolmen and some deputies from the local sheriff's office were fanned out alongside the road between - Fred Billings's house and the Curtis home. We were retracing the steps of Ian Curtis based on information provided by Kevin Bottoms, the last person to see him before he disappeared.

Just after the national anthem, Ulster had gotten on the P.A. system and announced that one of our students had gone missing, that classes were to be dismissed for the day, and that all students were encouraged to join the sheriff's department on an immediate search for the boy. Most of the kids didn't know who Ian Curtis was but they were excited about being involved in a search for what might turn out to be a dead body.

The school buses took us out to the Curtis house. My father organized the search. He was already out there when I stepped off the bus. I didn't want to join the search but I knew I had to, being the son of the sheriff.

"We're searching for Ian Curtis." My father was holding up a Xeroxed picture of Ian. He was talking to a bunch of kids on the side of the road. "I want you all to join Deputy Quinlan and he'll give you instructions from over there." He had his hand on my shoulder when he said it.

We were all shuffling through the arid desert brush keeping our eyes on the ground. I was walking beside Deputy Quinlan. Every time we took a step a swarm of grasshoppers would fly up from where it looked like there was nothing but sand. It was a sickening sight, hundreds of kids fanned out across the desert staring at the ground, searching for a body, the sky awash with grasshoppers.

My father had enlisted the help of a couple of his buddies from the Nevada highway patrol. A lot of them hung out at a bar on the north end of Las Vegas called Scoundrels. It was a cop hangout. Monday nights were what they called Meet and Cheat nights. The cops, most of them married, would go there with the intention of getting laid. Some of the strippers from the Olympic Gardens went there as well. Scoundrels was where my father had met Kimmy. I remember her telling me once that she liked cops, that they turned her on. Even though she didn't strip anymore and was working respectably for the city of Carmen, she still liked to flash herself in front of me when my father wasn't looking. She had a tattoo over her left breast that read

Johnny Forever. I was depressed for days when I saw that. Kimmy was the type of person who you could just tell was getting her heart broken on a regular basis. Every day she had to climb out of the shower and see the name of some guy she'd pledged to spend her life with tattooed on her chest. And when she was stripping she must have had every yank asking her how Johnny was. One time when Kimmy and my father were fighting I heard him say, "So then why don't you go back to that guy on your tit?" My father hated tattoos. I just think they're a bad idea, I just think if you're going to get a tattoo, don't get the name of a loved one, get those thorns that wrap around your arm or maybe a skull — get something that's going to be around a while.

I could see my father talking to Ian's parents at the edge of the road. Mrs. Curtis was wearing a pair of jeans and a T-shirt and she actually looked sort of composed. This time Mr. Curtis was doing most of the talking. It looked to me like Mrs. Curtis was in shock and Mr. Curtis was just trying to keep it together.

I noticed Mary sitting in my father's squad car. She was crying. There was a refreshment truck set up on the side of the road and Deputy Carol Ceirley was buying a soda. She took it back to my father's squad car and gave it to Mary and I watched Mary say, "Thank you."

My father was so calm that I almost didn't believe he had spent the night getting rid of a body. It didn't seem possible. I kept trying to imagine how else Ian could have disappeared from the trunk. Mrs. Curtis was holding on to his arm again. He was pointing down the road and motioning east to where Fred Billings lived when the dogs arrived. I guess one of the deputies had called the Las Vegas police department to see about borrowing some dogs from its K-9 unit. Some officer from McCarran Airport had brought a couple of German shepherds, which I guess they used as drug sniffers.

The airport cop got out of his car and let the dogs out of the backseat. My father walked over and introduced himself and the Curtises. Mrs. Curtis handed the cop a T-shirt that I guess had belonged to Ian. The cop held it in front of the dogs while they sniffed it, then he took it away, then he held it in front of them again.

All of a sudden both of the dogs started sniffing my father's shoes and growling at him. They were growling and barking and they wouldn't stop. The cop had to hold them back before they attacked my father. He was apologizing to my father as he dragged the dogs back to his cruiser, climbed in, and drove off toward the airport.

Just then, Deputy Ronald Stokely drove up. He was nearly as big as my father and had also played college ball before going to the police academy. He was probably my father's best friend. He was always calling my father Captain, and whenever he saw me it was "Captain Junior, what's the good word?" He also had the best complexion I'd ever seen on a man. One time he told me that it was because he had such an active sex life with his wife. Police work hadn't jaded Stokely the way it seemed to do to other people. Stokely got out of his car and went over to my father to show him something on a piece of paper. Then I watched him walk over to Benny Jericho, who was trudging through the desert with his head down. That was when I knew what was on the paper: it was a list of everybody that Kevin Bottoms could remember from the party the night before.

Stokely said a few words to Benny and then they both started walking back to the cruiser. My father stood waiting for them. He opened the door, letting Benny get into the backseat. One by one, we were going to be questioned. We were going to be asked who else had been at the party and if we remembered seeing Ian Curtis there. We'd be asked to tell everything that we could remember and then we were going to be asked what we thought might have happened to Ian. It was standard procedure whenever somebody went missing to ask the last people who'd seen him what they thought might have happened to him.

Benny Jericho was answering Stokely's questions. He said something that made Stokely glance up at my father and made my father scan the desert until his eyes fell on me. I knew that Benny had told them about the wedgie. When my father looked at me I turned my eyes back to the ground and continued walking.

"Can you believe this?" It was Reed. "That was the kid from last night, the one you gave a wedgie to." I gave Reed a look. He wasn't aware of how loud his voice was.

"I know who he is," I mumbled.

"I wonder if he's dead."

"I don't know," I lied.

We walked for a while in silence, searching the ground for Ian.

"I just don't get it."

"What?"

"You're this close. You're this fucking close to getting everything you wanted." Reed was trying to understand why I was quitting the team. I didn't know what to say. I didn't have an answer for him.

"So he would have walked this way," said Reed. "Didn't you leave right after him?"

"I don't know."

"Yeah, you did."

I stared at the ground. I could feel Quinlan looking at me. Reed's voice could really carry out there in the desert. I forced my face into Reed's direction and fixed my eyes on his forehead.

"Well, I didn't see anybody."

Quinlan went back to searching the desert floor but Reed was staring at me now with his mouth open, his eyes racing like crazy all over my face. And then he pulled away and forced himself to stare at the ground like he couldn't look at me anymore, like he'd just heard something that he wished he hadn't.

It got very quiet as everyone fell into their own private thoughts and the steady buzz of grasshoppers just gradually blended into the landscape.

It was a shock when Grace Daly started screaming.

Everybody looked up and saw her recoiling from something that she saw on the ground. She was waving her hands in front of her like she was shaking water off of them. Suddenly everybody was racing over to see what they expected would be Ian. They tore across the desert as if somebody had just dropped a bundle of money from the sky. I looked over and watched Mrs. Curtis — she had her hand over her mouth and was sobbing as if she already knew that her son was dead. It made me think of my mother. Did she wonder if I was alive and whether I was OK? I pictured her in my mind, in the laundry room, folding her pantyhose. I tried to see her face. I tried to see her smiling at me, see the love in her eyes, but I couldn't. It was just a blur.

"Dead dog," Quinlan yelled up to my father. My father waved a hand back and nodded. "OK, everybody back to your places, let's go."

I watched Grace step gingerly around the dog and continue walking. She was nervous now. Most teenagers never think about death and so to suddenly be confronted with what you eventually must face, to see it staring right back at you. It made her scream.

12

ONE BY ONE, everybody who was at the party was taken up to the cruiser to be questioned and then sent home. They were all sent home because my father didn't want them corroborating their stories with the people who - hadn't been questioned yet. The last thing a detective wants is people making up stories.

Occasionally I caught some of their looks. They were all telling Stokely and my father what I had done the night before. They had no reason to lie for me. They told my father about how I had given Ian a wedgie, about how I had humiliated him.

The cruiser inched along the road beside us as we walked all the way to Fred Billings's house. At lunchtime they fed us hot dogs and cold sodas. Me and Reed walked together in silence. Reed usually talked a lot but that day he didn't have anything to say. It seemed like he was trying to match my stride but he couldn't. And it made me feel guilty, responsible, like my stride was somehow defective, impossible to match.

And then Stokely came to get us. We were the last ones to be questioned.

"Reed."

Reed didn't look up. He just followed Stokely back to the cruiser with his eyes fixed on the ground like he was still searching for Ian.

He got into the back of the cruiser with my father. I watched my father and Stokely talking to Reed, asking him questions. Reed was nodding and then he started to speak. I tried to make out what he was saying but he was too far away. I wondered if he was telling them about seeing me on the road the night before.

"Don't worry, you'll have your day in court." It was Quinlan.

"Pardon me?"

"You keep watching 'em. Don't worry, they're gonna get to you."

I turned back to the desert floor and continued walking. I was terrified that Reed would tell them about our encounter on the road, that it would become clear that he had caught up to me and that I must have stopped somewhere on the road. I knew that if he told them that, I'd be history.

Reed's folks pulled up behind my father's cruiser. My father got out of the car with Reed and walked toward them. He shook Mr. Banks's hand and began chatting with him like he was his best friend in the whole world. I could feel myself starting to shake. I suddenly had this urge to run and join Reed's parents. Terry and Dot. Those were their names. They were the kind of people who you couldn't imagine ever not having been together, the kind of people who would live to be a hundred and then die within days of each other. Even their names fit snugly together. Terry and Dot.

Reed's mother was the most beautiful lady I'd ever met. It was the way she said my name. Nee-all. It made me blush. She dragged it out into two long syllables as if it just thrilled her to say it. Me and Reed would walk in the door and he'd announce, "Neil's here," and she'd say, with this big beautiful smile, "Hi, Nee-all," and all the blood would rush to my head. A lot of times when you go to some kid's house his folks look at you like they're half expecting you to steal something from them. They make you so nervous that you find yourself looking around actually wondering what it is you *could* steal. Reed's mother never made me think about stealing.

They lived on Constellation Boulevard, an endless street of drab, cheaply built houses with scorched lawns and no vegetation. I'd never been to Bakersfield but I couldn't imagine why anyone would *choose* to move to Constellation Boulevard.

Me and Reed would go in the backyard and play. At dinnertime Mrs. Banks would tell me that I should call my father to see if I could stay for dinner. I hated asking him if I could stay for dinner. I was always scared that he would say no.

"The Bankses invited me for dinner and Mr. Banks said that he can drive me home."

"What do you say after they feed you?"

" 'Thank you.' "

"That's it." And he would hang up.

I remember the first time my father met Mr. Banks. As Mr. Banks's car pulled up in front of the house my father came out the front door. I watched him as his eyes fixed on the parade of homemade tattoos up and down Mr. Banks's arms; he bristled for an instant before his familiar puzzled grin returned.

"Hi, I'm Terry, pleased to meet you."

"Chester." They shook hands. "Thanks for feeding my boy."

"No problem." Mr. Banks reached down and mussed my hair and my father bristled again, this shudder, like he was catching his breath — except that I could feel it in my bones. It scared me. I didn't understand why I felt terrified when my father saw Mr. Banks muss my hair, but I did.

I was the last one to be questioned. Stokely walked toward me.

"How you doing?"

I nodded.

"We need to talk to you."

I walked with Stokely toward his cruiser. My father sat in the backseat staring at a sheet of paper in his hand. He didn't watch me approach. He didn't look up until I'd sat down beside him. Stokely sat in the front seat and let my father ask me the questions.

"You were at that party last night?"

"Yeah."

"Did you see this boy there?" My father showed me the Xeroxed picture of Ian.

"Yeah."

"You want to tell us what you did to him?" I froze. I didn't know what to say. I wanted to ask him the same question. ". . . What you did to him at the party?"

"I gave him a wedgie."

"Pardon me?"

"A wedgie."

My father sat there and didn't say anything for a long time. "Do you remember seeing him leave?"

"Yes."

"And you threw a beer bottle at him?"

I nodded. I wondered who'd told him that.

"And you left shortly after him?"

"Yeah. Yes."

"Did you see him on the road?" My father was staring at his notebook when he asked me this. Stokely was gazing at me, waiting for me to answer.

"Did you see anyone on the road?" Stokely's forehead was creased, waiting for an answer. Was he asking me about Ian? Or was he asking me about Reed, checking our stories to see if they matched?

"No." It came out like a whisper.

"You're sure?"

"Yes, sir."

My father sighed heavily. "What do you think happened to this boy?" My mouth was dry. I couldn't speak. I just shook my head. "Any ideas?" I shook my head again. "OK, get out."

And that was it. It was over. Was it possible that Reed had kept his mouth shut about seeing me on the road? What was that look he'd given me when we were searching the desert? Did he know? I knew that I could never ask him.

I felt like I was watching my body from a distance as I floated over to the refreshment van. Nobody knew anything that they could pin on me except that I'd given Ian a wedgie. It wasn't a crime. We were always doing that sort of thing. Mary lifted her hand and waved wearily to me from the cruiser as I drifted past her on my way to get a soda.

We searched until it got dark. My father stood on the side of the road and blew a whistle. We all shuffled toward the road and stood around silently. Nobody felt much like speaking. I'd heard somewhere that when Saint Bernards went out with a search party and couldn't find the victims or if the victims were dead they became very depressed. We were all standing around like Saint Bernards, looking bewildered. Mr. Curtis was hugging his wife and daughter. Some of the girls were crying and hugging each other and most of the rest of us were staring at our feet as if we were still looking for Ian.

Off in the distance I could hear a buzzing like a high-tension wire, steadily growing louder. There's a U.S. Air Force base just outside of Carmen as you head south into

Vegas. Once a month they'd fly night patterns, relying solely on their instruments. They'd fly right over you in the darkness and the roar from the engines would be so deafening that you'd duck because it felt like they were going to slice your head off.

A shiny Ford eased onto the gravel shoulder. A man in a gray windbreaker got out and began walking toward the rest of us. When Mrs. Curtis saw him she ran from her husband and began hugging and jabbering to him, but the jets were so loud that I couldn't hear what they were saying. The jets were roaring directly overhead and everybody was ducking and holding their hands over their ears but my father never lifted his gaze from the man in the gray windbreaker. The bump on my father's forehead was beginning to turn red. And that was when I knew that the FBI had arrived.

13

H IS NAME WAS Clive Burden and he was Mrs. Curtis's brother. He was average height with a brush cut, and his face appeared tense but expressionless. She had called him that morning in Philadelphia and he'd gotten on the noon flight to Las Vegas, rented a car, and driven to Carmen to be with his sister and see if he could help in any way.

Mr. Curtis shook hands with Burden and then introduced him to my father. My father didn't flinch, just shook his hand and said, "It's a pleasure to meet you." Burden looked very calm. Even as Mrs. Curtis started breaking down, he asked Mr. Curtis and my father some questions about the investigation. He stood with his feet planted and listened with his chin out and these intense eyes that stared far away at nothing that I could see. I moved in closer and watched my father trying to match Burden's easy cool, but the bump above his right eye was turning a bright crimson.

The buses had arrived and the remaining students were slowly climbing aboard. My father waved me over and introduced me to Burden. We shook hands. He smiled and said that he was pleased to meet me.

My father put his hand on my shoulder and said, "Would you mind taking Mr. Burden's car and driving Mrs. Curtis and Mary back home?"

Mrs. Curtis and Mary sat in the front seat together, holding hands. Neither one of them was crying now. Mrs. Curtis tried to make conversation.

"Mary tells me you're on the football team."

"Mom!"

I didn't know what to say. We drove in silence for a while.

"Are you a senior?"

"Yes, ma'am."

"What do you plan to do . . ."

She was going to ask me what my plans were after high school, but then she stopped. In midsentence she changed her mind; I don't think she wanted to hear about anybody's plans. I pulled into their driveway and stopped the car.

"Thank you. Would you like to come in?"

"No, I'll just walk home from here."

"OK. Thank you." Mrs. Curtis wasn't going to force me to come in. She probably couldn't have cared less about what I did. She was just trying to be polite. "Mary, I'll be inside." She got out of the car and went into the house.

"God, I can't believe this. I know it's going to end up that he just went to Las Vegas or something. He's always doing stuff like that. He never tells my parents where he's going. Last night when she said his bedtime was nine, I just wanted to laugh. He did this one time when we were living in Mississippi and my mother called the police. It turned out he'd met some kid whose parents played in a dance band at one of the casinos. Ian spent the night hanging out with this kid and then sleeping in his family's hotel room. The parents worked all night so they didn't even know until the next day around noon that Ian was there."

I was really having trouble hearing her talk about Ian. Every time she said his name I felt this pounding in my head. She kept talking about him like he was still alive. I wanted to tell her that he was dead. I wanted to tell her that they'd never have to worry about his running off again.

"I just wish I knew where he was."

"He'll turn up." I didn't know what else to say. She just seemed so scared that I wanted to make her feel better. I wanted to give her some hope. It was an awful thing to do. And that was when she started crying. I put my hand on her back and rubbed it until she slowed down and was just sort of whimpering.

"My mother didn't want to move here. My father made her. She wanted us to stay in Mississippi. She said we had roots there."

"It's OK," I told her. And that was when she casually put her arms around me and squeezed me tightly. I said it again: "It's going to be OK." She wasn't crying now; I could feel her relaxing. I could feel her hard breasts against my chest. We were both sitting there in the front seat rubbing each other's back and then I felt her hands creep up to my neck and she started running her fingers through my hair and digging her nails into the back of my scalp.

"You're sweet," she said. I knew it was wrong but I didn't stop her. She was kissing my neck, soft little kisses on my neck, and then she started kissing my cheek, very slowly, barely touching the skin. And then we were kissing on the lips and she put her tongue into my mouth. I reached under her T-shirt and put my hand on her breast. I could feel her nipple standing up. I ran my hand over her breast and then I squeezed her nipple and she started to groan. And then she was rubbing her hands all over me. She was rubbing my legs and sticking her hand up my T-shirt and touching my bare chest. We kept kissing as I pulled up her T-shirt and unhooked her bra. I pulled it away and I put my mouth around her nipple and worked my tongue back and forth. She reached down and undid my jeans. She shoved her hand down inside my pants and started touching me and I put my hand down her and I could feel her soaking wet. I moved her onto her back and she pulled up her skirt and slid off her panties. She helped me pull my jeans off and I lay on top of her.

She didn't say a word as I entered her. She just lay there and exhaled slowly and dug her nails into my shoulders. I moved slowly back and forth, in and out, and then I started to quicken.

"Go slow." She was gently stroking my head. "Yeah, yeah, yeah."

I knew it was wrong, I knew it was a mistake, but some part of me just didn't care. The way she was touching me and moving her hands all over me, I lost control.

She was running her fingers up and down my back when suddenly the whole car lit up. There were headlights shining in the car. I pulled myself away from her and tugged at my jeans while trying to stay out of sight. It was my father in his squad car with Mr. Curtis and Burden. Mary pulled her clothes on.

"Damn, damn, damn," she was saying.

My father must have been talking to them because the lights just stayed on us and we didn't see anybody walking to the house. Then Mr. Curtis was walking past the car with Burden. He saw me and knocked on the window. I wound it down.

"Thanks," said Mr. Curtis. At first I didn't know what he was thanking me for.

"Oh, no problem, sir."

"Would you mind opening the trunk?"

"Pardon me?" My heart stopped.

"Mr. Burden's luggage is in the —"

"Oh."

I popped the trunk.

"Would you like to come in for dinner?"

"Oh no, sir, that's fine, I . . ."

"We can drive you home after."

I didn't know what to say. He was smiling at me as if he were eternally grateful for all the help he'd gotten from my father and me. I didn't want to appear suspicious and so I smiled back at him and said thanks. We climbed out of the car, me and Mary. As I closed the door I glanced across the car and saw that the two men were watching me. I turned away as I pulled up my zipper. We all walked toward the house together, the men letting us go first — I knew they were just being polite, but I couldn't help thinking that they were keeping an eye on us.

The Curtises had one of those L-shaped living rooms that adjoin the dining room. There were a lot of boxes in the living room. Mr. Curtis explained that he had just picked up supplies. There were boxes of candles and plastic flowers, and in the corner he had a stack of plastic Jesuses that were piled almost halfway up to the ceiling. I could see they were constructed in a way that they could be easily stacked — they sat next to a pile of brown plastic crosses painted to look like wood. The Jesuses had two holes in their backs where they got screwed to the crosses.

All the furniture was brand-new. It reminded me of hotel furniture: it was hard — it appeared comfortable until you sat down and within a few minutes were squirming around searching for a position that would let you relax.

I could smell roast chicken and potatoes and suddenly I felt hungry. We all walked into the kitchen. Mrs. Curtis was bent over the counter furiously chopping some vegetables, and I could tell that she'd just been crying.

"Mary, why don't you give Neil and Uncle Clive a drink," she said.

"I'll just have a water, thanks," I said.

"I've asked Neil to stay for dinner," said Mr. Curtis to his wife.

Mrs. Curtis looked at me as if she were happy that I'd changed my mind. Mary gave me a glass of water and Burden a grape juice. Burden went over to Mrs. Curtis and practically whispered in her ear.

"Mandy, I need some plastic baggies."

"OK."

"I want to isolate some of Ian's personal stuff."

"OK."

Mrs. Curtis gave Burden a roll of little plastic bags. Mr. Curtis walked up the stairs with Burden to show him which items belonged to Ian. I stood in the kitchen with Mrs. Curtis and Mary. All of a sudden we heard Burden upstairs, yelling, "No, don't touch that!"

Burden came out of Ian's bedroom carrying some of Ian's personal effects in baggies that he put into a briefcase. Mr. Curtis walked behind him guiltily, as if he were the one who had run over Ian.

I went into the living room with Mary. She ran her hand through my hair from behind me as I walked to the couch. We sat down and she was staring at me like she couldn't believe I was in her house. I could hear the adults in the kitchen. Burden was asking the Curtises questions about whether Ian had any enemies or if he spent a lot of time on the Internet and then I heard Mrs. Curtis whisper, "Shh . . . I don't want to upset Mary with this." Mary looked at me and rolled her eyes and from then on we couldn't hear a thing they were saying — it was just this forbidden buzzing that only gave you a headache if you strained to listen.

Eventually Burden came in and sat on the couch across from me and Mary. We just sat there, not speaking. Finally I said, "How was your flight?" He looked at me and nodded. He was pale, as if he'd never been outside in the sun before. His skin looked like water; it was blue and paper-thin and seemed to be stretched too tightly over him. It was almost as if you could see right to his insides.

He just sat there sipping his grape juice. I guess he wasn't the sort of person who spoke a lot. Finally Mary said, "Uncle Clive, how's work going in Philly?"

He looked at Mary and smiled. "It's doin' fine. How 'bout yourself, you working hard in school?"

"No, not really."

We sat down for dinner. There were only four chairs at the table and so they gave Burden one from the living room. There was a little video game on the table in front of me. When I saw it I realized that I was sitting in Ian's chair.

We all joined hands while Mr. Curtis said a prayer. He asked God to give his family the courage and strength to accept whatever was His will. And then Mrs. Curtis began to cry. At first I didn't know if she was crying, it sort of looked like she was laughing, her face was tense and she was holding her knuckle over her top lip. Her knuckle was turning white and suddenly I felt guilty because I realized that she was holding back her tears because of me. She didn't want to cry in front of a guest. She got up from the table and went into the kitchen. I think we were all waiting for Mr. Curtis to go and comfort his wife, but he didn't. And so Burden did. I could tell the exact moment when Burden put his arms around his sister because that was when she started sobbing these really loud gasping sobs.

Mr. Curtis put his knife and fork down and sat there staring at his hands, and so I did the same.

"You don't have to stop." Mary was telling me that I didn't have to stop eating, but I just wasn't hungry anymore. She wanted me to feel comfortable but the more she tried to make everything all right, the more I just wanted to run screaming out of the house. And so we sat there, me and Mary and her father, staring at our hands while Mrs. Curtis stood in the kitchen sobbing in her brother's arms.

14

MR. CURTIS OFFERED to give me a ride but I told him I'd walk. Mary came outside with me. When we got to the edge of her driveway she tried to kiss me but I pulled away. "I'll see you tomorrow," I said. She looked sad. "Are you OK?"

"No."

I wanted to get away. I wanted to start running down the road, I wanted to just keep running past my father's house, right through Carmen, and keep going. I wanted to run to Alaska until the air froze my lungs and pinched my face, until I woke up from all of this.

The road sloped off sharply so I stuck to the pavement and when a car drove past I stepped into the ditch. I didn't like walking in the ditch because of the snakes. They were very common, especially at night. When I was eleven I'd gotten bitten by a small rattlesnake. It's over before you know it and then the snake's gone and you're just left rolling around on the ground screaming for your life.

I walked through the darkness listening to the jets flying overhead. The Penguin's older brother Nathan had been in the Air Force. He'd flown in a war a few years earlier protecting some country from some other country, though I can't remember which ones. Two weeks after coming home he'd gotten in an argument with some guy at a bar in Vegas and when they'd taken it outside the other guy's buddies had jumped him and now Nathan got around in a wheelchair. Nathan had been a bigger danger to himself on leave than he'd been alone up in his plane dropping bombs on industrial parks.

I kept thinking about my father and how he'd gotten out of the car and shaken Mr. Banks's hand. It made me angry. I remembered the night that they first met out on the driveway — the night when my father saw Mr. Banks muss my hair. He had just broken up with this lady Carol who was a cocktail waitress at Caesar's Palace. Lately he had been glaring at me when I came home from Reed's house. I didn't play football with him anymore and now he was all alone. We went into the house and he mixed up a pitcher of Green Russians and proceeded to get wasted. I went up to my room. I'd asked him once if I could put a lock on my door, but he wouldn't let me. I could hear him downstairs wandering from room to room like he was retracing his steps, imagining how he could have done things differently with Carol.

After a while I heard him climbing the stairs to my room.

He was in a rage. He acted like he was calm, like he wanted to have a father-son chat, but I could tell that he was just looking for a reason to explode. He told me that he didn't like the Banks family. "He's got no self-respect, desecrating his body with those tattoos." He told me that Mr. Banks didn't know how to be a father and that he didn't want me hanging around *them people*. "Like father like son," my father said, which scared me more than anything. He told me that Mr. Banks had been in prison and that he was a con. It was true. Reed's father had been a con. Reed had told me that his father had served five years and eight months in a California prison for armed robbery and that that was why they'd left Bakersfield, to make a new start.

The following day at school I tried to avoid Reed but it's difficult when you're in the fifth grade and sit next to each other. I knew I shouldn't believe my father but I looked at Reed differently after that. I wondered if he was going to become a con. I wanted to hate him but I couldn't, there was a part of me that just didn't care if he became a con. He was my best friend. When he'd told me that his father had gone away for almost six years and then come home again, it made my heart race. Reed had given me hope that a parent could return.

That night I went over to Reed's house and we practiced throwing the ball in the backyard. When Mr. Banks drove me home I asked him to stop at this ramshackle convenience store a half mile down the road from my father's house. I told him that I needed to pick up some stuff for my father and that I would walk home. After a few weeks, my father had a new girlfriend and he didn't notice that I was gone all the time but I made sure that Mr. Banks never drove up to the house. I was terrified of his ever meeting my father again, terrified of what my father might say.

Occasionally Reed just wanted to play in the backyard, race around and spray me with the water hose, but now playing terrified me. It was irresponsible. I didn't want Reed to become a con.

And so we practiced.

We ran patterns and grass drills. I took a stopwatch from the school and clocked Reed's times for the fifty. I pushed him to work on his speed and yelled at him when he dropped the ball. He would look at me in confusion as if he didn't understand what was going on, but I couldn't explain it to him. I couldn't explain that I was trying to save him from a life of crime.

As I approached my father's house I could see that the light was on. I couldn't see my father or Kimmy, but I knew they were home. I slowed down and listened to the gravel crunching under my feet. I listened to the crickets and I breathed in the cool, dry air, exhaling it slowly. I put my hand on the doorknob and turned it. And the first thing that I heard was laughter.

15

THEY WERE BOTH LAUGHING.
    "No! Stop it! Stop it!"

My father was chasing Kimmy around the living room.
I stood at the side door, listening. I wondered if he was
ever going to mention Ian to me. I wondered if he was just
going to pretend forever. I didn't know what to think. He'd
been drunk the night before. Was he having regrets about
what he'd done now that he was sober? I wondered if
he even remembered what he'd done. I walked to the entrance of the living room and watched them. Kimmy was
on her back, giggling, while he sat on top of her, tickling
her ribs.

"Stop it!" She was laughing the way she used to when
they first started dating, and so was he, laughing this low
sort of chuckle. There were a couple of glasses on the coffee table. The ice was almost melted in them. My father

looked at me and smiled. I stared back at him until his smile went away.

"We saved you some meat," he said. I guessed he hadn't heard yet about my quitting the football team.

"The Curtises fed me." I said this right into his eyes. I didn't care how far I had to travel, I stared deep into his eyes to see if I could catch a glimpse of the end of the road.

"Nice folks," he said as he stroked the back of Kimmy's head. Kimmy was watching us and could sense the tension.

"There's some pie in the fridge," she said, like maybe pie might help.

"I'm gonna do some homework."

I walked upstairs. I put on my headphones and cranked up Nirvana. I was listening to the song "tourettes" on *In Utero*. I didn't understand anything Kurt Cobain was screaming. It sounded like

COLD HEART! COLD HEART! COLD HEART!

I stared at the photograph of my mother. Her name was Honey. I looked at the letter she had sent me on my birthday when I was five.

> Dear Neil,
> Happy birthday! I want you to know that I love you very much and so does your Daddy. I'm sorry I won't see you but you be a good boy and know that your Daddy loves you very, very much.
>
> Love Mommy

It was a strange writing style. All the *y*s ended with these fancy curls that just sort of lifted up at the end and took flight, nearly running right off the page. I don't know why but it made me think of all the men who milled around the entrance to the Hollywood Theater before Neil Diamond's shows. They had that look, as if they'd received letters just like mine. I could see the letters written all over their faces. They were familiar with those final exits where the door shut behind her and you could practically hear her sigh of relief. It killed me that I recognized that look because I hated those men. They scared me. Abandoned, lost forever, trying to keep their heads above water and sinking slowly as if somebody were underneath pulling at their feet, as if they were taking their last gasp before the world swallowed them up and spat them into the ground. Neil Diamond made them feel for those brief ninety minutes that they mattered or maybe just that they existed — that they were present and accounted for. His songs were personal battle cries from the pit of his belly, all wrapped up in sequins and schmaltz. They knew they could never be Elvis but surely they all had a shot at being Neil Diamond, a skinny Jew from Brooklyn, the greatest lounge act on earth.

My father was roaring with laughter now. Roaring out of control like he was trying to convince himself of something that he used to believe a long time ago. It was a laugh of recollection. He was roaring and she was giggling and they were doing their best to pretend that they weren't terrified of each other.

Sitting there on my bed, I understood his laughter. He

was relieved. He controlled me now. He had buried the body and now we shared a secret. We were linked by Ian Curtis and now I could never be free again. I could hear him downstairs roaring with relief.

As I stared at the photograph of my mother, I could feel her staring back at me. She was disappointed. She was turning and walking away, walking out of the picture, until all I could see was a three-year-old boy with his arms in the air and nobody holding him up.

She was gone, but I couldn't accept it. I needed to believe that one day the front bell would ring and I would open the door and she'd be smiling back at me. That she would embrace me and we'd start to laugh and all the pain would disappear. In a single instant it would be gone and I would get into her car and we'd drive away. We'd drive to where I threw the fifty-four-yard pass. I'd show her the place where I first kissed Lenore. I'd show her all the places where I had gone and tried to hold on to my innocence. And then I'd show her where I killed Ian Curtis on the road and she'd take me in her arms and tell me that I was forgiven. Maybe she'd even tell me that it didn't really happen, that none of it happened, and that it was all just a dream. And then we would drive away from Carmen, drive for days until the past faded into the distance and I didn't feel alone anymore. Just keep driving until we disappeared into thin air.

TUESDAY

16

MY FATHER WAS TAPPING the steering wheel and humming along to "I Think It's Going to Rain Today," from Neil Diamond's 1971 MCA record *Stones.* He was driving me to football practice. I hadn't told him that I'd quit, I didn't know how.

He was slowing the car down. I noticed Burden's car parked up ahead on the side of the road. As we pulled over I saw the skid marks and deep gouges in the gravel that I'd left two nights before. Burden was walking slowly around in circles in the brush. He was wearing a worn golf shirt and khaki pants and a stupid-looking explorer's hat that I could tell he'd borrowed from Mr. Curtis to keep the sun out of his eyes.

"Stay here." My father got out of the car and walked toward him. I wound down my window. Burden looked up as my father approached him; he looked angry, as if he were trying to control himself.

"Good morning," said my father.

Burden spread out his arms as if taking in the desert. "This is a crime scene," he said. "Those kids had no business being out here on a search."

My father bristled at this. I didn't have to see his face to know that the bump on his forehead was turning red. Burden was pointing at something on the ground. He had a trowel and a Tupperware jar. He took the lid off the jar; inside was a rock.

"This is blood." He had found Ian's blood. "And look at this." He was pointing to the skid marks and the gouges in the gravel. "See, they've trampled this whole area. Who knows how much evidence you've lost."

My father stood there defenseless. He had done it on purpose. He had wanted to destroy any evidence that might be here. He had used the Carmen High student body as accomplices.

Burden was pointing to a couple of footprints that ran diagonally to the ones from the search, footprints that approached from the road.

"They may have come from the person who killed . . . whatever this was."

"Most probably an animal."

Burden got really quiet. He stared at something in the distance, then turned to my father and said, "How many people kill an animal and then get out of their car and take it with them? There's no sign of an animal's body. Just blood. And it hasn't been dragged away."

"Well, let's check this out." My father reached out to take the Tupperware container from Burden. Burden pulled back.

"I've got a guy in Vegas who'll do it," said Burden.

"I think you'd better give me that container." They stared at each other for a minute. "I strongly suggest you hand me that container, Mr. Burden, or I will cite you for obstructing justice." Burden stared back at my father with a look of curiosity. He stood almost a full head shorter but his gaze never wavered. Finally he handed my father the Tupperware container. My father began walking back to his car and now Burden was following him.

"This area should be cordoned off."

My father spun around and faced Burden. They were standing right in front of my father's car. "I think it would be a real good idea right now for you to stay out of my business," my father said.

Burden's glance fell to the front of the car.

"Your signal light's broken."

My father looked at his left-turn signal light, cracked from the impact of Ian's body. He stared at it for a moment, then dragged his attention away, got back into the car, and placed the Tupperware container on my lap.

"Hold this."

I could feel Burden's eyes watching us as we pulled back onto the road and drove away.

*   *   *

We turned into the parking lot of the school. Some of the other fathers were standing around and talking with each other by the front doors. All their heads turned as my father and me got out of the car.

"Hello, gentlemen." My father shook some hands. The men were squinting at me.

Mr. Jericho spoke up. "This is a surprise."

"How's that?" said my father.

"I thought he left the team."

My father's head snapped in my direction. Just then Ulster came out of the school and walked toward us.

"How are you, Chester?" Ulster got along really well with my father.

"Well, I'm not sure. I only just heard."

Now they were all looking at me but I didn't have anything to say.

"It's a cryin' shame. No disrespect, Chester, but I think your boy was a little under the weather yesterday and we may have had a communication problem." My father looked at me, studying me as if this were news to him, wearing this look of shock and concern. "If Neil still wants to play, then perhaps we can bury the hatchet and forget the whole thing. We got a big game on Saturday and we need to start acting like a team."

It wasn't that I didn't love football. I did. Throwing a completion into the end zone was the dream that put me to sleep at night. It was what made me feel as if I existed. And maybe that was it. Maybe I didn't want to exist. Maybe I didn't want to feel anything that made me more aware of my sins. Playing ball only reminded me that I'd killed Ian Curtis. I just wanted to be like all the other kids. I wanted to be innocent.

I couldn't look at the men. They were giving me a second chance and I was defying them. I was holding them hostage with my decision and they hated me for it. Especially my father; if we had any connection, it was football. All I could think about was the extra money he spent on meat for me. Football was what kept me fed and clothed. I played to keep myself alive. As long as I threw a good game, I knew that I'd be safe a little longer, but I just couldn't do it. And so I said no.

As my father got into his car I turned, and he was staring at me. Something cleared away in his eyes and for a brief second that faraway look vanished and all I saw was fear. I thought it was my imagination but I couldn't shake it. He looked frightened. As if he were afraid of . . . what? Me? It didn't make sense but that was what it looked like. Like my father was afraid of me.

I walked down the hall, keeping my eyes on the floor as I passed some of my teammates on their way out to practice. The school was empty. At the end of the hall I could see the janitor mopping the floor. He was an old man with heavy lines on his face. It occurred to me that I'd never heard him speak to anyone. Every day he mopped the floors or painted over the graffiti and we marched right past him. I thought about all the damage that I'd created for him to clean up — I remembered the time I'd scribbled all over the toilet stall with a felt marker. He never complained. He never even spoke. He just came in with his brush and painted over our messes. I wanted to thank him, to apologize for all the trouble I'd caused, but as I got closer I could feel myself getting uncomfortable. Maybe he'd think I was making fun of him. I suddenly started feeling extremely self-conscious about scribbling all over that toilet stall. As I walked past him he looked at me and I turned away.

I walked past my ninth-grade locker. I remembered my first day at Carmen High. I was nervous and so I picked a fight with some other kid because he bumped into me. I wanted everybody to know how tough I was. I didn't want people to think that they could fuck with me.

There were footsteps behind me. I turned and saw Stokely walking toward me with Mrs. Doyle, my ninth-grade homeroom teacher, and Mr. Curtis.

For a second I thought that they knew, that my father had told them and they were here to arrest me. That wasn't fear I'd seen in my father's eyes, it was fury — he was fed up with having a son who didn't do as he was told. He would happily clean up my mistakes if only I did him one small favor, if only I played ball. And now I had betrayed him and it was over.

I noticed that Stokely was carrying a pair of metal snips.

"Good morning, Neil," said Mrs. Doyle.

"Hi."

They stopped at a locker right next to my old one.

"This is it," she said. Stokely raised up the snips and chopped off the lock.

Mr. Curtis looked exhausted but he kept his head up. It was almost as if he were telling himself consciously to stand up straight even though he just wanted to sleep for days. He looked me in the eyes and I could see that he knew about the wedgie. He didn't say anything. He just looked sad. He had taken me into his home, fed me, and treated me decently, and now he knew how I had treated his son.

I turned away and slunk down the hall. They were looking for clues in Ian's locker, something that might indicate his whereabouts. I knew that they would find nothing in his locker to indicate his present situation. I knew that Stokely was just carrying out my father's instructions.

I sat in the library staring at the clock, waiting for the bell to ring. A couple of students walked in; they were laughing and the librarian told them to be quiet. There was a book about Oregon sitting on the table and the pictures made it look beautiful, with its forests and coasts and big open spaces. I imagined taking a bus to Oregon and getting a job in a lumber mill, just blending in and changing my name. I was thinking about what I would change my name to when Lenore walked into the library with Jill Menzies. I pretended to read my book until she sat down next to me. I was ready to hear her tell me what a jerk I was for quitting the team and how she didn't want to see me anymore. Or maybe how she didn't want to see me anymore because of what I'd done to Ian Curtis the other night.

"Hi," she said. She was wearing a white T-shirt and a blue skirt. Jill wasn't with her now so I knew that Lenore had something to say. She wasn't the kind of girl who just ditched her friends whenever she saw her boyfriend.

"Hi."

There was a long, awkward pause. "I've been thinking a lot about the other night," she said, "and I think that maybe we should . . . you know."

I stared at a picture of Oregon. I stared at the trees and I pictured myself way up in one of them, far away from Carmen.

"Say something," she said. She was holding my hand. "Neil, what's wrong?"

"Nothing," I said.

"I thought this was what you wanted," she said. How could I tell her that things had changed, that I couldn't have her anymore, that it was all wrong? "Neil, I love you." She was squeezing my hand. "I don't care if you play football or not. I'm your girlfriend, and I love you and I always will. I just want you to know that." I wanted to start crying when she said that, but I didn't, I just kept staring at the tree in the picture. "Say something," she said.

"I don't know what to say."

Jill Menzies was watching us while pretending to read her book. I sat there with Lenore, not speaking, and I held her hand.

"It's going to be OK," she said. And the way she said it, I almost believed her. And then I surprised myself. I lifted my head up and looked into her eyes and I was about to tell her that I loved her too, but when I saw her eyes I couldn't do it.

"What were you going to say?"

I wanted to get away. I wanted to be up in that tree so badly. Why was she doing this? Didn't she understand? I just wanted to be left alone. She had her hand on my leg. She was rubbing my leg and I just felt numb. I kept remembering the way she'd looked at me as she went into the kitchen with Amy and now here she was forgiving me, offering herself to me. I thought about Mary. I thought about what I'd done with her the night before and my eyes started burning. Lenore wanted to sleep with me and all I wanted to do was run. I hated her for being so forgiving. I hated the world for forgiving me over and over again until it was too late. I blamed everybody who'd ever looked the other way from my behavior. I blamed them all for Ian Curtis's death. I'd been getting away with murder for years before the Curtises ever even showed up in Carmen.

17

I SAT IN HOMEROOM. Clyde and Dayton were at it again, whooping and carrying on. Mrs. Aemes told them to shut up and I just tried to ignore them. During the morning announcements Ulster said a prayer for Ian Curtis and his family. Some of the students were talking about where Ian might be. I saw a couple of girls in the hall crying and talking about how awful it all was, but it already felt different. We were back in school. The novelty was gone. None of the kids wanted to shuffle through the desert with their heads down for ten more hours. Nobody really knew who Ian was and they all figured the chances of their finding a body and being a hero were getting slimmer by the minute.

I'd heard Ulster's prayer before. It was basically the same prayer he gave us before we played a game. He talked about how the good Lord had a plan and wanted the best for all of us and sometimes when it felt like we couldn't go on we needed to reach out our hands to Jesus and let him carry us those last few yards. He finished with that psalm that goes, as I walk through the valley of death, I shall fear no evil. By the end of his prayer a lot of the kids were crying and Mrs. Aemes was crying harder than anybody. She told us how much she loved us and said that it wasn't possible for a person to teach kids and not love every single one of them. She was one of the few teachers who could say something like that and make it sound believable.

She got us to move our desks into a big circle so that we could take turns talking about loss. I excused myself to go to the bathroom when Debra Ives started talking about how she'd lost her brother who was a jockey. He had died at the Belmont racetrack. He'd gotten boxed in and his horse had panicked and tried to jump another horse. Her brother had flown off his horse and broken his neck and died instantly. Debra told the class that she didn't blame the horse. That was when I had to get up and leave. The horse her brother had been riding was called Bugaboo. She said it like it was just information, and I almost expected Mrs. Aemes to point out the wonderful irony.

I went to the bathroom and sat on the toilet. My head was throbbing and I was having trouble breathing. I tried to relax. I felt the way I did when it was a close game and the clock was counting down and I was looking for a way through the defense. But I was already safe. My father was the sheriff and he'd gotten rid of the body. He was careful. I didn't need to do anything. I just needed to sit in class and listen to everybody talk about loss. I just had to sit there and pretend that I wasn't a killer.

I walked back into the classroom while Tracey Beckwith was talking about her dog Justin. Justin had died of old age. Everyone sat patiently as Tracey told us about Justin, who was a mutt that she'd gotten from the Carmen Humane Society when she was six. Tracey Beckwith had red hair and was almost six feet tall. She was big-boned and splattered with freckles. Some of the students used to tease her and call her Big Red. I was one of them. The previous fall, Tracey had attempted suicide by swallowing a lot of her mother's diet pills. While she was in the hospital there'd been a school meeting in the cafeteria with all the students and teachers and it had been made very clear that if anybody said anything to her that could possibly be construed as negative then they would be suspended. Since then everyone had stayed clear of Tracey except for a few kids who were overly nice to her. It was disgusting. Before her suicide attempt nobody had wanted to sit with her in the cafeteria and now people were inviting her to sit with them and even giving up their chairs. I just don't think there's anything worse than being treated like you're special. I'm not condoning calling somebody Big Red but what made me angry was that most of the teachers were hypocrites. They didn't care about Tracey any more than we did, they just needed a scapegoat and it was a lot easier to blame the students than to acknowledge the real problem. One look at Tracey's family would tell you that her mental instability had begun long before anyone ever thought of calling her

Big Red. I remember seeing the way her father kissed her when he dropped her off at a dance. I remember stealing glances at her in health class when the teacher talked to us about *improper touching* — she looked like she was in the middle of a London fog. After seeing the way her father kissed her I could hardly blame her for wanting to inhale a bottle of diet pills.

By the end of the class everybody was crying and I felt as if I were the one who had killed Tracey's dog and Judd Greely's uncle and Heidi Miller's grandmother and Debra Ives's brother. I felt as if I were the one responsible for all the tears. I sat there with my eyes dry, staring at my hands and hating them all for being allowed to express their pain. I wanted to tell them about loss. They didn't know about having somebody walk out the door and then just never hearing from them again. I could tell them a thing or two about loss. Me and the Curtises both.

18

I KNOW ULSTER'S a hardass, but don't you see what you're doing?" Reed had grabbed me as I was heading into the cafeteria and insisted that we talk. He was sitting in the driver's seat of his '75 Plymouth Fury and gesturing dramatically at me with his hands. "Ten years from now you won't even remember him and you'll look back on this as the biggest mistake . . ." He kept talking about Ulster as if he were trying to convince himself that Ulster was the reason I'd quit the team.

Reed's father had rebuilt the car and given it to him for his sixteenth birthday. It was this midnight-blue eight-cylinder monster with a 318 engine and a fully restored interior. Mr. Banks had taught Reed how to maintain it, how to change the oil and do a full inspection — he was very patient, making sure that Reed understood each step. My father wasn't much for lessons. One time he woke me up in the middle of the night and tried to teach me how to shave. I was twelve. I doubt he'd even remember it, how I held him up while he slathered the shaving cream on my face. I told him I wanted to sleep but he said that he was preparing me to be a man. He kept telling me that I could ask him anything. "Ask me anything," he kept saying, like there was something he desperately needed me to know.

"I just don't want to play anymore. I just don't."

I couldn't look at Reed and so I stared at the plastic UNLV football key chain that hung from his rearview mirror. I'd given it to him five years earlier, bought it in Vegas for ninety-nine cents after a Neil Diamond concert. The day his father gave him the car he drove over to my place and there it was dangling from the mirror. I hadn't even known that he'd kept it. I wished he hadn't. Blown by the air conditioner, it was swinging back and forth like a pendulum and it was starting to give me a headache.

"But this is all we've talked about. I mean, what about . . ." I knew what Reed was going to say before he said it. "What about me and you?"

It was the first time that he had mentioned it. I wanted to pretend that I didn't know what he was talking about, pretend that he was making it up. I wanted to scream at him, *"Don't you know what I did?"* But instead I just repeated myself. "I don't want to play anymore."

"And this is because of Ulster?"

I was getting frustrated. I wanted to tell him yes but I knew that he wouldn't leave me alone if Ulster was the only reason for my quitting the team.

"No."

"Well, then, why?"

Why? It was a question I could never answer. I didn't have a reason, at least not one to satisfy Reed. But I gave him one anyway. "Because of my father." We never spoke about my father but Reed had seen the way I got quiet around him, the way I became tense when I talked to him on the phone. "He's been pushing me my whole life and I'm sick of it. I'm sick of doing whatever he tells me to do. I just don't want to play anymore. I just want to be left alone." I couldn't understand why it sounded empty. All of it was true but when I heard the words come out of my mouth they just sounded silly. I didn't know what it was, but I knew that he didn't believe me.

"And that's it?"

"What?"

"That's why you're quitting?"

"What? Why?"

"Don't you see what you're doing? You're throwing away your life because you're angry with your father."

I remembered the way my father had shut the trunk and strolled back to the Curtises, all calm authority and nothing the matter. And then the body was gone. It terrified me. I didn't know what my father was capable of. I kept hearing him telling me to stay away from *them people* and suddenly I realized that he hadn't been referring to the Bankses. *Them people* meant everyone but him. He wanted to control me, control my life. But why? What was he afraid of?

"It's like you've got all these secrets and you just don't

tell me anything. I mean, I don't even know if we're friends anymore." Now Reed was staring at the plastic football key chain. "We used to be best friends." I didn't know what to say and so I just ignored it.

"But I told you."

"I just want to know what's going on. I feel like I did something wrong."

"You didn't do anything wrong."

He pulled a sheet of paper from his pocket and handed it to me. "Here." I began unfolding it. "Look at it later." I put it in my pocket. Reed let out a sigh. "I know about that scout giving you the jacket." I could feel my face turning red. "I just don't see how you can throw that away. This is what you wanted. This is what you've been working for. I just don't understand why you didn't tell me."

"I . . ."

"Neil, I didn't tell anybody about seeing you on the road." I tried to swallow but I couldn't. He was going too fast. I felt like he was coming after me now, like he was going to run me over. I looked out the window and watched a couple of guys tear up a textbook and throw the pages into the air. I watched the pages scatter across the parking lot. "Your father and Stokely asked me if I'd seen anybody on the road Sunday night and I told them I hadn't." The air conditioner was going full blast but I could feel the sweat collecting on my eyebrows. "I didn't tell anybody." And then he turned and looked at me. "Nobody knows." I stared at him.

"It's not . . ." I was trying to laugh, trying to make it light, but I was squeezing the door handle and suddenly the door popped open and I nearly tumbled out of the car.

"Are you all right?"

"Look, I just gotta . . . I gotta get . . ."

"I didn't think I'd catch you on the road. What were you doing? I mean, did you stop to piss or something? I've been trying to think of . . ." He turned away from me again. ". . . What did you do?"

I wanted to tell him, to just push the words out of my mouth and know that it would be OK. I glanced at him then and suddenly I was walking back to the school. I could feel Reed's eyes on me and I felt extremely self-conscious, afraid that any misstep would give me away. A stabbing pain shot through my gut from where Ernie Gates had jabbed me the other night. Some students stood by the door smoking cigarettes and watching me as I approached. Their faces were just a blur as I pushed open the metal door and walked back into the school.

19

I WAS FIGHTING against the rush of bodies on their way out of the cafeteria and it happened before I had time to think. Mary was walking toward me with this expression like she was in the middle of some torturous experience and I was the only one who would understand. She looked so lost and anguished that I opened my arms and it was only after I was hugging her that I realized everybody in the cafeteria was watching us — the football team, Dayton and Clyde, Fred Billings, Amy and Lenore. And I could tell by the looks I was getting that Mary had told somebody about last night and now it was all over the school. Everybody knew about what we had done in the front seat of her uncle's rented Ford.

"How are you doing?" I asked her.

"I don't know," she said. She was holding back her tears and trying to be strong. Everybody in school knew who

Mary Curtis was now, and it was clear from her eyes that she liked it.

I could see all the other girls watching Mary, wishing that *their* brothers were missing. She was the most envied girl in school. She had the sympathy of the entire student body and nobody could say anything bad about her. She was someone to be supported or at the very least pitied. The other girls were beginning to flutter around her, handing her tissues when she got misty and holding private conferences with her in the bathrooms.

She was wearing a lemon skirt with a matching jacket. She wanted her pain to be dignified. She wanted to set an example for the other girls. I remembered the *A&E Biography* on the JFK assassination that had been playing on her television two nights before, and I realized that Mary was trying to be Jackie Kennedy. Here she was in her mother's outfit playing the role of the sorrowful sister.

I felt like a prop, the guy she'd chosen to turn to for support. I was her man and nobody could call her a slut or say that she had stolen me from Lenore. She was grieving and couldn't be held responsible for her actions. What had happened between us the previous night was entirely my fault; I had seduced her — taken advantage of her when she was vulnerable. I don't know how long I stood there holding Mary and wondering what to do. It was as if she'd changed overnight: yesterday she'd been a skittish, awkward teenager and today she was a sophisticated charm-school graduate, well versed in the etiquette of public grieving.

"Please sit," she said, like she was hosting a wake.

She was sitting with Paula Bell, Judy Moffitt, and Julie Sorge. Paula and Judy hung out together. Paula had gone out with Reed the year before. One night Reed had gotten drunk and Paula had found him messing around with Beth Henderson. Paula refused to take him back. Reed still talked about what a huge mistake he'd made. At parties he usually ended up getting drunk and crying about it.

"Hi," I said to the other girls.

"Hi, Neil," they all said back. Julie Sorge looked uncomfortable and out of place, sitting there in her shiny green halter top with tassels. It was only a matter of time before she got the hint that Mary had new friends.

"Any news?" I asked Mary. She shook her head. She was very calm, like she didn't know how to react, like she was playing a role and didn't know all of her lines.

"Thank you for last night," she said. The other girls looked away as if we were sharing something intimate. I nodded my head. I didn't know what else to do.

I noticed Lenore talking with Amy. I knew what they were saying. They got up together and walked out of the cafeteria.

I'd lost my appetite. I didn't know how to get away from Mary. I felt guilty. If I left I'd be a jerk, but if I stayed then the rest of the school would know it was true. Finally I looked at my watch and told her that I had to run. She nodded her head as if she understood. She didn't care, her job was done, everybody in school knew that we were involved and that I had messed around on Lenore. And I had proven it. That hug in the cafeteria was not a mistake. Mary had been waiting for it all day.

I walked out of the cafeteria. I could feel the stares: I was the guy who had mysteriously quit the football team and was now involved with the girl whose brother was missing. I was going to look for Lenore but then I changed my mind, I just didn't feel like lying anymore. I just didn't want to deal with it. I went to the library and pretended to look at books in the back aisle. I liked it back there. It was quiet and empty. I'd fooled around with Lenore back there a couple of times but this time I was hiding. I wanted to get away from everybody.

I saw a book called *The History of Villains.* I opened it and was reading about all the great villains, like Al Capone, Jesse James, Babyface Nelson. At first I didn't see Lenore. I didn't know how long she'd been standing there as I stared at an old picture of the FBI's Ten Most Wanted. I imagined my face being on that poster. I imagined Burden calling up his bosses at the bureau and telling them that they had their man. I imagined him coming to our house and telling my father that he would have to arrest me and my father nodding and letting him in.

"Is it true?" Lenore was holding back tears. I could tell she was about to start crying.

"Is what true?"

"You and that . . ." She was about to call Mary a slut but then she remembered that her brother was missing.

"What did you hear?"

"That you slept with her."

"What?" I was very calm. I didn't trust myself to act indignant. I didn't have the energy.

"That's what I heard. That's what she told Judy Moffitt."

"Well . . ." I wanted to tell her the truth, about Mary, about Ian. I wanted to apologize for everything. "Well, it's bullshit," I said.

"Then what happened?" Lenore didn't want to believe that I'd slept with Mary. I knew that she was going to believe whatever I told her.

"After the search, I drove her and her mother home. She was upset so I gave her a hug." I decided to stop there, just not even mention that I'd kissed her.

"And that's it?"

"That's it."

"You didn't kiss her?"

"No." I looked right into her eyes when I said it. I didn't feel a thing. I didn't feel the old excitement of fear or panic, the way I used to when I lied to her. I felt nothing. It almost felt as if I were telling her the truth.

20

I WAS SITTING in Mr. Russell's class writing my name at the top of the algebra test when I glanced out the window and saw my father getting out of his cruiser. At first I didn't recognize that it was Burden he was with.

I saw my father's face in the window of the classroom. He knocked and then opened the door. He shook Russell's hand and told him that I needed to be excused.

We walked in silence to the far end of the school. He held a door open for me. It was the music room. Burden was sitting on a chair in the middle of the room. He stood up when I walked in and motioned for me to sit down beside him. My father stood against the wall.

"I just want you to know that you're not a suspect or anything. I just have a few questions that I'd like to ask you."

"OK."

"I know you were at the Billingses' house the other night, the night Ian went missing," he said.

I nodded.

"Do you remember Ian being with another boy, Kevin Bottoms?"

"Yeah."

"And can you tell me what happened?"

My father stood against the wall, staring at me.

"Well, I'd had a couple of beers and when they showed up I guess we got kind of rough with them."

"Who's 'we'?"

"Me and the Penguin — uh, Craig Nutt."

Burden nodded. "Had you ever had an altercation with Ian or Kevin before?"

"No, I'd never talked to them before."

"Do you remember them leaving?"

"Yeah, they were running down the lane, I gave Ian a wedgie and I guess they both wanted to get away." I'd decided to tell him about the wedgie because I knew that his questioning me meant he'd seen the police report.

"And when did you leave?"

"I guess I left about twenty minutes later."

"Do you remember passing either one of them on the highway?" When he asked me this I looked over at my father. I couldn't help it. My father stared right back at me, right into my eyes, like he was testing me. I waited for a sign, for him to nod, to tell me what to do. Did he want me to tell Burden the truth? He just stared grimly back at me, waiting for me to respond. And that was when I understood what he was doing. There was no reason for Burden to be questioning me. This was my father's investigation. He hated the FBI. He was letting Burden question me because he wanted to see me sweat. He was letting me know who was in charge.

"No, sir, I didn't see anybody."

Just then my father moved away from the wall.

"Thank you for your time," said Burden. I realized that the interview was over. My father had ended it. He had been controlling it the whole time.

As we stood up, Burden said, "So, what made you quit the football team?" I gasped when he asked it; he'd caught me off guard.

"I . . . I don't know," I sputtered. I realized immediately that this was the only question that Burden had really wanted to ask. Everything else had been just a pose to get in the room. "I just . . ."

Burden kept staring at me, waiting for me to finish. Finally my father stepped in. "Pardon me, Mr. Burden, but my son is in the middle of a math test. Let's save the chitchat for when we're all a little less busy."

I went back to class. I ignored the stares as I walked to my desk and pretended to work on the test. All I could think about was Burden. He knew. That question, "What made you quit the football team?" Even the way he phrased it: "What *made you* . . . ?"

I tried to concentrate on the test, but I couldn't. When I stared at the page the numbers just wiggled back and forth out of focus. The class was almost over and I watched the door for Reed. This was his free period and so he always waited for me by the door. He'd stand and wave at me through the window, but this time he wasn't there. I just wanted to know if I could trust him, if he could keep his mouth shut about seeing me on the road that night.

I sat at my desk waiting for the test to be over. I knew that I would get a zero; I'd tried to answer one of the questions but then I'd just ended up erasing it. There didn't seem to be any point — even trying a little bit felt like I was just putting up a struggle. It felt more dignified to hand in a blank page.

Mr. Russell was sitting at his desk studying somebody's test paper. He looked genuinely interested. He was smiling. We put him through hell and every day he kept showing up. I remember one time I saw him with his kids at the Carmen Recreation Center. They were competitive swimmers, a boy and a girl, skinny, with broad shoulders and clear dark-brown eyes. I couldn't believe that they belonged to this man. This scrawny, hunched-over man had produced these beautiful young age–group champions. He was with his wife, a pretty woman with a nice figure. I wanted to tell Mr. Russell that I was sorry for all the pain that I had caused him. I wanted to assure him that it would never happen again, but it was too late. Besides, he probably didn't even care. Sometimes I wondered if he even noticed us.

The bell rang. Mr. Russell told us to stop writing and hand in our papers. I picked up my pencil and wrote, "I'm sorry," at the top of the test. I dropped it on his desk and I kept walking.

21

I WALKED DOWN THE HALL wondering if Burden knew that his nephew was dead. He'd found the blood and seen the broken signal light. But I knew that they would never find the body. I turned the corner and saw all the usual students roaming the halls, and standing a head above them, talking with some of the girls, was my father. He couldn't help himself. He loved to be around females. And they loved him. We'd be sitting in a restaurant and he'd say to the waitress, "What're you asking for the trout?" *Asking!* Like it was negotiable. And the waitress would just start blushing from how charming he was. I don't even think he was aware of the effect he had on people; he just radiated this sense of security that made everyone a little giddy.

But when I saw him I froze.

He wasn't with Burden.

I spun around and began walking down the hallway as

fast as I could. I went into the library. Lenore looked up but I ignored her. I went back out the door and now I was running down the hall. Running to the music room.

Burden had seen the police files.

He was looking for Reed.

There were students watching me as I stopped at the door and peeked through the window, but it was too late: Reed was sitting with his back to the door and Burden was standing in front of him. They were tossing a football back and forth and Reed was speaking but I couldn't hear what he was saying. Burden appeared relaxed, like he had all the time in the world. He looked up at me and smiled and I turned away as if I'd been caught.

I walked back down the hall, my face burning. I heard somebody say my name but I didn't turn, I just kept walking until I found an exit. I just needed to get out of the school as quickly as possible. I needed to be alone.

22

I WALKED THE SIX MILES from school to my father's house. I waited for the buses to leave so that the other kids wouldn't see me. I waited around the far side of the school in this alcove where some kids were smoking, skipping their last period. At first I could tell they were scared and thought that maybe I was going to cause some trouble. They were younger than me — two guys and a girl, fat and pimply with paper-white skin from hours spent hiding from the sun in mall arcades and basement rec rooms.

I asked them for a cigarette. They were sneaking glances among themselves as I fought with their lighter. I took a deep inhale and as I felt the smoke go into my lungs I realized that there had been a knot in my chest all day, and as it loosened it felt like someone was pushing a dagger into my heart. I slid down the wall until I was sitting on the cement. I could see where all the kids had horked gobs of spit on the ground but I didn't care. I just sat there waiting for the pain to go away, then took another puff on the cigarette and started to cough. The smoke went down the wrong passageway and I felt as if I were going to choke.

I stood up and introduced myself after the coughing fit passed. The girl introduced herself and the two guys but they both turned away when I looked at them. One of the guys showed me how to inhale. I accidentally brushed against his arm and could feel his cold, wet skin. I took the smoke into my mouth, pulled it into my lungs, held it, and then let it just flow back out of me. I tried to forget about Reed. I kept seeing him talking to Burden and I didn't want to know what he had said.

We stood there until the bell rang. Before they left they gave me two cigarettes and their lighter. I stood there for a while playing with the lighter, turning it on and then snapping it shut. From where I was standing I could see the top of the goalposts and every thirty seconds I could see a football go flying between them where our kicker, Robby Stinson, was practicing.

After a while I put one of the cigarettes in my mouth and smoked it. I concentrated on the smoke going into my lungs and I thought about cancer. I wondered how long it would take to smoke myself to death. I remember how when Kurt Cobain killed himself, most of us were in shock but the Penguin kept telling everyone that Cobain had been selfish, that he had left a wife and kid behind, and that he was an asshole. I understand what he was saying but I just don't think anybody really wants to die. I think some people feel so hopeless that they probably think everyone is better off without them. I'm sure that was what Kurt was thinking. It makes me angry when I think about what the Penguin said. I think some people are just afraid to admit that they understand that kind of hopelessness.

I finished the cigarette and my throat was starting to feel dry and sore. I watched some men across the street unload lumber from a truck. I knew one of the guys. His name was Brian and he had played on the football team two years ahead of me. He was being loaded up with as much lumber as his shoulders could support. I wondered if he knew he'd be humping lumber from a truck back when he was scoring touchdowns.

I threw my cigarette against the wall and walked toward the street. I didn't want Brian to see me, but it was the only way home unless I walked all the way around the school. It didn't matter because Brian was too engrossed in his task to notice anybody. It looked to me like he was trying to impress the two older men he was working with by showing them how much lumber he could carry. I stopped about twenty feet from him, right in the open, and lit the last cigarette. I wanted him to see me now. I wanted him to see me smoking the cigarette, but he didn't, he just carried the lumber onto the construction site. One of the men looked at me and I gave him a thumbs-up. I was going to give him the finger but at the last minute I changed my mind.

*　　*　　*

I walked along the highway flicking the lighter on and off as cars whizzed past me. I kept flicking it until it stopped working and then I threw it into the ditch. I wanted to walk to Reed's house and ask him what he had told Burden. I wanted to ask him if I could trust him.

Our first year at Carmen High, I made the team and Reed didn't. He became the waterboy, getting up early to chop oranges and coming to every practice to cheer me on. I remember standing with him in the hall when the lineup was posted and his crying out "Yeah!" And when I saw that it was for me and that he hadn't made the team I wondered if I would have done the same.

I was thinking about all of this when I remembered the paper that he had given me in his car and I pulled it out of my pocket. It was a poem that he'd written called "Champions."

CHAMPIONS

To be the best
Is a quest
That never rests
To put our bodies to the test
And let our spirits lead the way
This indeed is the nobelest quest.

It was Reed, straight from his heart and filled with spelling mistakes. It practically made me want to start crying, but in my mind I kept watching him talk to Burden and I kept replaying our conversation in his car. "What about me and you?" he'd said. He was pinning his dreams on me and it made me angry. I wondered if he was as innocent as he pretended to be or if he was a con and my father had been right all along.

I crumpled up his poem and threw it into the ditch.

23

I WAS SLIDING MY FEET along the gravel and counting my steps when I heard a woman's voice. I looked up and saw a Las Vegas News van parked on the side of the road. A man in a sweaty T-shirt and cutoff shorts was filming a pretty blond reporter with a beta-cam as she stood on the edge of the road with the yellow police tape behind her. As I walked past them they were wrapping up, the man resting against the truck while the woman chatted with him. I smiled but they didn't acknowledge me, just glanced in my direction and then kept on talking as if I were some kind of apparition.

I was a few miles from my father's house when a car pulled over on the side of the road and stopped in front of me. It was Kimmy. I walked to the passenger door and got in. She was smoking a cigarette. She didn't look at me, she just pulled back onto the road and kept driving.

"He's going to be late tonight. They're working overtime looking for that kid," she said. I took a cigarette out of her pack and lit it with her matches. She glanced over but didn't say anything. We drove the rest of the way home in silence, smoking, with the air conditioning on and the windows up.

We went into the house and I went up to my room. I was pacing. I hated my room. It was really the attic. The sides of the ceiling sloped nearly all the way to the floor and so I was always walking into the walls with my head. I hated the view from my window. All I ever did was stare at this cactus. I'd been watching it forever, ever since I was a kid. It never grew. Every year it was exactly the same size.

I put on my headphones and shoved in Nirvana's *Incesticide* CD. I was lying on my bed listening to "Been a Son," trying to picture my mother's face and see the sadness, see the loss in her eyes and fix it to the only memory that I had of her, that moment in the laundry room, but I couldn't. Her face was a blur.

Kimmy was banging on my door. I took off the headphones.

"You have a phone call."

I picked up the phone in the kitchen.

"Hi, it's me," said Lenore.

"Hi."

"What are you doing?"

Kimmy walked into the kitchen and opened the fridge. I started to wonder what she was going to make for dinner.

"Are you there?"

"Yeah," I said.

"Do you want to come over?"

"I'm not feeling too good." Now Kimmy was looking at me. She wore the same resigned expression that she gave my father when she knew he was lying to her. "How are you doing?"

"Fine." We sat in silence for a minute. "If you don't want to see me you can just say so," she said.

Kimmy was taking food out of the fridge and putting it on the counter.

"I'm just not feeling too good." I wanted to tell her that we could get together on the weekend but I didn't feel like making any plans. Finally I just told her I'd call her back in a little bit and I hung up.

I walked out of the kitchen and then I stopped and walked back. Kimmy looked up, surprised; she was pouring herself a glass of Midori.

"If anybody calls for me, tell them I'm not here."

"Where are you going?"

I wasn't planning on going anywhere. "For a walk."

I went into my father's office. It was a small room in the corner of the house that he hardly ever used. I sat behind his desk and stared at the phone. I couldn't stop thinking about Reed in the music room with Burden. I tried to push it out of my mind. I thought about Lenore but that only made me depressed and then I thought about Mary and then my father and then the team but no matter what I thought about, it always led back to Ian and there was no room in my head for anything calm. And so I picked up the phone and dialed Reed's number. It rang once and I hung up. I stared at the phone, half expecting him to call me back. I let my hand hover over the phone as if it would ring at any moment and I would pick it up very casually and ask him how he was doing. Finally I just dialed his number again and let it ring. Even as it was ringing I knew I was making a mistake.

"Banks residence."

"Reed, it's me." I waited for him to respond, but he didn't. "I was looking for you after algebra."

"Yeah. I didn't wait for you." He was in the kitchen. I could hear the television in the background and his mother washing dishes in the sink. Mrs. Banks used to slice up these green apples and cheddar cheese and bring them to us on Sunday afternoons while we watched the game.

"I was looking for you."

"I know, you said that."

I wished I hadn't called. I wanted to tell him to go to the phone in his parents' bedroom. I didn't want his mother hearing us talk.

"How was practice?"

"It was all right."

"Who's quarterback?"

"Cullen."

"That's what I thought."

"Hey listen, I gotta —"

"No, I just want to say . . ."

I really regretted calling. I wanted to tell him that I'd

made a mistake. I was hoping that maybe he would volunteer some information, but he didn't.

"So . . . where did you . . . where . . ."

"I was just around."

"Oh." He didn't want to talk. "'Cause I was looking for you."

"I know, you said . . ."

"Well, fuck . . ." I tried to sound angry but not too angry. I wanted him to know that I was still his friend. I was getting scared. I wanted to tell him that I'd seen him with Burden. "Look, you really made me think about a lot of stuff today . . . and I wanted to thank you . . . and I want you to know that I'm not going anywhere without you. I mean that. We're a team." I didn't even know what I was saying. I wasn't used to Reed's not speaking — usually I was the one who was silent — but he didn't have anything to say so I just kept talking. "I really liked your poem. It really helped me to make some sense out of all of this. And . . . I just wanted to say thanks."

"I better go. I got practice in the morning."

"Hey . . ."

"What?"

I wanted to remind him of how his mother had sliced up those apples for us, and how we'd sat on his couch for hours passing the football back and forth and watching TV. I wanted to apologize for all the times that I'd yelled at him when he dropped the ball. "Nothing."

And click. He was gone.

I walked back into the kitchen. Kimmy was sitting at the

table, massaging her foot with one hand and sipping her Midori with the other.

"How come you're not at football tonight?"

"I quit."

At first I wasn't sure if she'd heard me.

"Why?"

"Tired of it."

She didn't say anything for a while. She'd peeled off her pantyhose when I was in my father's office and now they were sitting on the floor in a little ball.

"So, how's work going?" I asked.

"Shitty." She stopped massaging her foot. "What do you mean, 'tired of it'?"

Suddenly I wanted to tell Kimmy about Ian. "I just don't feel like playing anymore."

I couldn't look at her. I wanted to tell her, make her understand that it'd been an accident, but instead I mumbled something about having to do homework and went up to my room.

When my father first started courting Kimmy, he'd bring her over and make her dinner and they'd watch TV together and laugh. I could hear them from my room upstairs. And then it'd get real quiet. Sometimes I'd stand by the stairs and watch them fool around. One time I watched him nail her in the living room. There was light coming from the TV. They were watching *An Evening at the Improv,* and he was bent over her, moving up and down really slowly. I watched her lying on her back, her fingers digging into his work shirt. His pants were around his knees and he still had his boots on. He looked like he was doing push-ups, like I'd seen him do when I was a kid. They weren't speaking — they weren't making a sound. As I watched them I felt sick and lonely but I kept watching, I couldn't pull myself away. When my father finished, his body stiffened and then he dropped down on top of her. He didn't kiss her, just lay there while she stroked his hair. I watched them for a while and then I went back up to my room and sat on my bed until I guess I fell asleep.

I was lying on my bed thinking about Kimmy. I put "Been a Son" back on the CD player and put on my headphones. Kimmy had long, silky-smooth legs and an ass like a pear. Her hair was unnaturally blond and she had a voice that was sexy in a sleazy, girlish sort of way. Even dressed in her business suit she was the kind of woman who you wouldn't be surprised to find out had been a stripper. I'd fantasized about her before even though it made me feel sort of dirty. It wasn't as if she were my mother, she was just my father's girlfriend. I don't know why, but I got really turned on by imagining being with her. For a while I imagined finishing what I'd started with Mary but then I had to go back to thinking about Kimmy — thinking about Mary just made me depressed.

I was lying on my bed staring at the ceiling, wondering about Kimmy and anything else that might take my mind off of Burden and Reed, when the front doorbell rang.

24

"NEIL. DOOR FOR YOU." I was pulling my pants back on as Kimmy called to me from downstairs.

I knew it was Burden. He was standing at the front door, sunburned and tired-looking. It wasn't until we sat down at the dining room table that I realized I was being ambushed. Burden knew that my father was still at work. He said that he just had a couple more questions. I thought about telling him that I wanted to speak to a lawyer but I decided not to.

"Do you want something to drink?" The words scared me when they came out of my mouth because I didn't know where they were coming from.

Kimmy was standing on a stool in the kitchen reaching into the back of a cupboard. I watched Burden eye her quickly from the back. She pulled out a tin of these fancy European cookies that I'd never seen before and put a few of them on a plate. She walked into the dining room and held the plate in front of him. "Well, you got some sun."

"No thanks." He waved them away.

Kimmy put the plate down as if she'd been wounded and disappeared out of the room. Burden sat facing me, his face and arms now a dangerous red.

"People make mistakes," he said. "They do something . . . foolish, something they regret. It doesn't make them bad people." I tried to swallow, but I couldn't. "It happens all the time. And then later, they admit their mistakes and they're forgiven."

I couldn't believe how red he was. I sat there wondering how long it took to die from skin cancer. He was sitting with his hands out on the table and I could see his pulse beating on his wrist.

"Do you understand what I'm saying?"

I nodded.

I heard a rustling sound — it was the sand coming in through a tear in the plastic sheet. I suddenly noticed how much sand had collected inside the house: there was a ridge almost a foot deep against the wall. I hadn't noticed it in such a long time, I'd blocked it out, but now watching Burden stare at the sand I could feel my face getting hot. My father usually replaced the plastic every six months but this time it had been over a year and the tears were growing all along the edges. I suddenly realized that my father was never going to finish the job. He was just going to continue to replace the plastic forever.

I realized, sitting there, that I had never had friends over to visit. Not Lenore, not anybody. Even Reed sat in the car when he came by to pick me up and I was always waiting by the door. Burden stared at the sand for a long time, puzzled, as if he were processing it, deciding something for himself. And then he pulled his eyes away from the sand and began to speak.

"Sometimes we panic . . . and sometimes the people we love give us bad advice." I could feel his eyes trying to connect with mine but I just kept staring at the pulse on his wrist. "Neil, I'm trying to be your friend. I want to be your friend here. Do you understand what I'm saying?"

"Yes, sir."

"You can call me Clive."

"OK."

"Is there something you want to tell me?"

"No."

He looked at the sand some more. "I'm Ian's godfather." His eyes looked sad. "When he was a year old he got very sick — scarlet fever — there were complications and . . . he was in and out of the hospital for two and a half years." In the reflection from a window, I could see Kimmy watching Burden, the smoke from her cigarette circling in thin wisps above her head. Burden had his face in his hand like he was trying to be a cop about it, but he was crying. "There were times when they didn't know if he would live or not. When I think of what his mother went through . . . it wasn't even that he might die, it was the waiting." I reached out and put my hand on his shoulder. I couldn't help it. I knew that my father would have done the same, he was always touching people. When I touched him he reached up and grabbed my hand. He looked up and he wasn't crying anymore. His eyes had red rings around them but his face looked tense, not loose and relaxed like faces usually look after somebody cries. "I know he's dead." My hand was starting to hurt but he wouldn't let go. For the first time I could see how strong he was. "After twenty-four hours we stop looking for a missing person and we start looking for a body. Did you know that?"

I nodded.

"I don't want them to spend any more time waiting. Do you understand me?"

I nodded.

"So why don't you tell me what happened?"

My heart was beating against my shirt and I wondered if he could see it. I wondered what Reed had told him. Burden just sat there staring back at me, calmly waiting for an answer. I glanced down and saw how quickly his pulse was racing.

"I don't know what you're talking about."

Just then the door that led to the garage opened and slammed shut and my father stormed into the house. When he walked down the hall he made the house shake, reminding us all of where we were. He flew into the kitchen carrying his briefcase, yanked open the liquor cabinet, and pulled out his bottle of Midori, trying to open it by twisting the top over his left forearm. He opened another cupboard and pulled out a glass using the same hand that his briefcase was in. The glass slipped from his hand and smashed on the counter.

"Ah, for Jesus . . . !" He threw his briefcase into the corner and stared at the broken glass. "Kimmy!" He grabbed another glass and began filling it. "Kimmy!" I glanced at Burden and saw that he wasn't watching my father — he was studying him. My father looked up and saw us staring back at him. When he saw Burden, he acted as if it were the most natural thing in the world for him to be in his house. He came into the dining room and shook his hand.

"What are you doing here?"

"Just asking your son some questions."

"Uh-huh. Well, in the future I suggest that you ask for permission before doing something like that."

"Your son is a suspect, Sheriff."

"A suspect." My father sounded surprised, as if he weren't aware that a boy had gone missing. "For what?"

"For killing my nephew." It made me cringe when Burden said it. For a second I didn't know what was going to happen. My father was glaring at Burden but Burden just held his gaze.

"I suggest that you get out of town tonight or I'll arrest you. This is not a federal investigation and I've put up with all I'm gonna take." And then he added, "Besides, how are you going to charge someone for murder without a body?"

"You mean *you*." Burden was shaking with anger. "How are *you* going to charge someone? Isn't that what you mean?"

"Get out." My father said it matter-of-factly, as if he were tired and just needed to go to bed. I sat at the table and watched Burden turn away from my father and walk out of the house.

25

I COULD HEAR HIM downstairs, wandering from room to room, his thoughts darkening, his judgment becoming impaired. Kimmy was in the living room watching television and I was up in my room staying out of the way. And then he started talking, quietly at first — he was asking her for something and she was valiantly trying to stand up for herself.

"I'm trying to watch television!"

"And I'm trying to talk to you!"

I heard the television getting louder as she tried to drown him out. And then there was a crash, followed by a violent silence — he'd put his foot through the TV set.

He beat up Kimmy that night. And I sat in my room and listened, terrified, and did nothing. I could hear her agreeing with him but it wasn't enough, he wanted something from her that she couldn't give him, he wanted something that I don't think he even understood.

I paced my room, one part of me hoping that Kimmy would get out and another part wanting her to stay so I wouldn't have to face him alone. I wanted to get his gun and make him stop but I knew I couldn't kill him and so I sat on my bed, frozen, listening to her struggle. I held the photograph of my mother in my hands and thought about how lucky she was for getting away. I didn't hate her. I knew that she'd done what she had to do and that she couldn't have taken me with her. He would have gone after her. I stared at her handwriting, girlish and pretty, each word ending with a dramatic sweep, the *y*s and *g*s flying up and away as if she were in a state of suspended joy. And the way she crossed her *t*s, right through the middle with a broad swipe. It was a strange writing style; one time I'd thought about getting it analyzed by a specialist to find out more about her personality, but I never did.

Kimmy was pleading with him to stop now. Begging him to leave her alone. She was screaming, "Let me go! Let me go!" And there was no sound coming from my father.

I climbed into bed and closed my eyes. I listened to my breath and I tried to let the screaming fade into the background. I could hear the resignation in Kimmy's voice as she screamed. I couldn't block it out and so I pretended that it was the television. I pretended that it was the middle of the afternoon and I was lying on the Bankses' living room couch, napping, and I could hear Mrs. Banks in the kitchen watching one of those afternoon talk shows. The ones where they tell all of their dark secrets and throw things at each other and you're laughing because you know that it's all just make-believe. I lay there and pretended that Kimmy and my father were on television and I drifted away. I floated out through the window, gliding along and hovering over the desert while the wind whispered secrets in my ear that it didn't hurt to hear.

And then I woke up and everything was quiet except for the sound of my father's footsteps coming up the stairs. I glanced at the baseball bat in the corner of my room. I grabbed it and sat up in bed. My father stood at the door and looked at me. "Give me the bat." I handed it to him and he placed it gently on my dresser. "You're playing ball to-morrow."

That was all he said, and then he was gone. His beating up Kimmy had been a warning to me. If I knew what was good for me then I would play ball. Kimmy lay in bed, battered, bloody, and all alone, shivering with fear, wondering why she had stayed with my father for so long. I felt bad for her but I also knew that she had a choice. She could leave. I could never leave. No matter where I went, I knew that I could never get away from him. Kimmy would continue to suffer as long as she stayed. That night had nothing to do with her. If only she knew that, if only she knew that she was suffering for my sins.

WEDNESDAY

26

M Y FATHER WAS HUMMING "Two-Bit Man-child" from Neil Diamond's 1968 album *Velvet Gloves and Spit*. It was 7:15 A.M. and he was driving me to foot-ball practice. We didn't speak to each other. There was nothing to say.

The locker room was dark, though I could feel that somebody else was in the room. I almost expected to turn on the lights and see Ian, like in some horror movie, all gory and dripping. It took me a second to find the light switch, then I turned it on and jumped back. He was facing the wall. He turned around slowly, as if he weren't surprised by the sudden intrusion, or maybe he was just too tired to care. It was Reed.

"Hi," I said.

"This guy from the FBI was asking me questions yester-day."

I glanced around the room to make sure we were the only ones there.

"He wants to know if I saw you on the road that night." He didn't even say "Sunday night." We both knew what *that night* meant. "He wants to know when I gave you your football hat."

I nodded, waiting for him to continue, but he didn't.

"And what did you say?"

"I told him that I gave it to you Monday morning after practice." Reed looked exhausted. He wanted me to say something but I couldn't speak. He had told Burden nothing. He'd kept his mouth shut. "Neil. I lied to him."

"It's OK." I didn't know what else to say.

"What do you mean?"

"Just don't worry about it."

"But —"

"It's over."

"But Neil, he told me that lying is a federal offense. He said that a person could go to prison."

"It's over," I said weakly.

"But I'm scared."

"It's OK." I didn't even know what I was saying. I wasn't making sense, I was just trying to fill up the air with words, to make everything all right.

"But Neil, I just need to know. I mean . . ." His eyes were racing frantically all over my face, looking for a place to land. "I need you to tell me . . . is it OK if I tell him the truth?"

I stared at the dark rings under his eyes. Reed never had

any trouble sleeping; when we were kids I would sleep over at his house on weekends and lie there beside him listening to his breath move in and out like a whisper. I'd try and breathe like him, hoping that maybe I could *become* him, that I could wake up the next day and Terry and Dot would be *my* parents and they would cook for me and love me and hold me when I was afraid. I never imagined that we traded places, though, I never imagined that Reed was me — I didn't want anybody to have to be me. But now I didn't know what else to do. And so I looked him in the eyes and I told him the truth.

"No."

He started to cry. I sat down beside him.

"It was an accident."

"Why didn't you tell me?"

"I was scared."

"But you can still . . ."

"No, I can't." I wanted to tell him about my father and why I couldn't tell the truth, but "It's too late," was all I said. Reed didn't say anything, and we just sat there not speaking until some of the players started walking in and we all began getting changed.

Fred Billings walked in with the Penguin. He sat down next to me and put his hand on my shoulder and said, "I'm glad you're back." I told him that I was sorry about what I'd said on Sunday night and that I thought he and Amy made a really good couple.

Ulster didn't make a big deal about my coming back. Before the practice he said something about having a "real complete team this year." During the practice I kept trying to focus, trying to push Ian out of my mind, but I couldn't, I was missing throws and dropping the ball. Now that Reed knew, everything was different. It wasn't a secret anymore but instead of feeling relieved I only felt worse.

After the practice I followed Reed out of the locker room. "It's going to be OK," I told him.

He couldn't look at me. He was staring at this bulletin board that listed all the activities for the rest of the year.

"His parents . . ."

That was all he said. He couldn't finish. He just walked away.

27

I WAS OPENING MY LOCKER when Lenore appeared, wearing these tight black pants and a shiny silver T-shirt with no bra.

"You didn't call me back last night."

"I'm sorry."

"No."

"Pardon?"

"It doesn't work, Neil."

"What?"

"I'm tired of pretending . . ."

"Of what?"

"That I love you . . . and hoping that you'll change."

"But I'm trying." I didn't even know what I was saying.

"I'm sure you are." She said it like she was sure I wasn't. "I don't trust you, Neil." And now she was crying. "I don't trust you."

I could feel the stares. "OK." I took my books out of my locker. I watched her walk away until, halfway down the hall, she just threw her hands up in the air like she was continuing her conversation with me and it was going nowhere. I wondered if she knew that I was watching her and if it was meant to make me feel guilty. I didn't trust her either.

28

I SAT IN CLASS and tried to pay attention as Mrs. Aemes had us all take turns reading from *Julius Caesar*. All the kids were laughing as Dan Hotchkiss staggered from desk to desk and we all pretended to stab him. It was on my stab that he decided to fall to his knees as the class cheered, and then he collapsed on his back, legs twitching, while Tracey Beckwith announced, "Liberty! Freedom! Tyranny is dead!" Everything was back to normal. It had been two days since the search and Ian was already forgotten. He was already old news.

I glanced out the window and saw a stream of cars, mostly Grand Ams and Monte Carlos, about a dozen of them, pull into the parking lot and men in suits climb out. All the heads turned and looked out the window and I felt this hot breath in my ear, "Killer!" I turned around to see

Dayton grinning at me and followed his eyes downward as a switchblade shot up from between his legs.

The FBI agents got out of their cars and chatted with each other for a few minutes before proceeding in pairs to the front doors of the school. Burden was there, dressed in a suit now and walking beside a very tall, gangly agent with thinning blond hair. Everybody in the class was chatting excitedly. "What do they want? Do you think they found him?"

There was a knock on the door. It was Mrs. Lowe, the school secretary, saying she needed Benny and Ernie and also Jane Evans, this red-haired cheerleader who had been at the party. Jane was friends with all the guys on the football team but went out with Ronald Predwinkle, a Carmen grad who was majoring in languages at Tulane. I waited for Mrs. Lowe to call my name but she didn't. Benny and Ernie got up and walked out with Jane. The door shut and I sat there wondering why they didn't want to speak to me.

Nobody felt like continuing with *Julius Caesar*, least of all Mrs. Aemes. She stood at the front of the class looking shaken, as if she were maybe going to cry again. And Dan had this expression of total remorse, as if he were embarrassed by his death scene, like it was somehow a personal affront to Ian's family. Suddenly everybody remembered that one of our students had been missing for three days and what had been funny two minutes ago was now something to be ashamed of. I wanted to scream at them that they hadn't done anything wrong. It made me angry that they felt guilty for something that had nothing to do with them. Dayton and Clyde were the only two who didn't seem to care.

Mrs. Aemes had this guilty look on her face as if surely there were something more she could do — and it wasn't like she could put our desks in a circle again. You can't just put desks in a circle every time there's a crisis — nothing would get done.

I felt the hot breath on my ear again. "Killer." I didn't turn around. I just waited for Dayton to stab me in the back of the head so that I wouldn't have to watch Mrs. Aemes looking guilty anymore.

Jane walked back in alone just as the bell was ringing. She glanced at me and when she caught my eye she turned away as if she might catch something if she stared at me for too long. I grabbed my books and walked out of the classroom. I wanted to tell Mrs. Aemes that she had nothing to feel guilty about but how the hell could I know that for sure?

29

THE HALLWAY was full of kids. All the students were quiet, as if somehow they were all suspects — as if they all had something to hide. I remembered the way drivers instinctively hit their brakes when they saw my father in his police car. He'd pull up beside them and they'd be staring straight ahead, gripping the wheel at two and ten o'clock just trying to look innocent, even when they hadn't done anything wrong.

Reed was standing in the hallway talking to Benny. Benny was asking him something and Reed was shaking his head. Benny turned and walked toward me. He glanced at me and then walked right past without saying a word. Reed saw me and motioned for me to follow him into the bathroom.

His hands were shaking. We waited for a couple of kids to walk out of the bathroom.

"They know you did it."

"Shhh."

"They're asking everybody about you. They want to prove that you stopped somewhere on the road."

As Reed was speaking I noticed a pair of feet under one of the toilet stalls. I held my hand up and Reed stopped talking. We stood in silence until finally the toilet flushed and this FBI agent stepped out. He left without washing his hands.

"Did they talk to you?" I asked.

"No. Benny wants to know what's going on. He asked me what the hell happened on Sunday night."

"And what did you say?"

"You know what I said. Neil, just tell them the truth."

"I can't. It's too late. Don't worry, it's going to be OK."

"It isn't fucking OK, Neil. He's dead."

I noticed that all of the toilet doors were open, all except for one, but there were no feet underneath it. I put my finger to my lips, telling Reed to be quiet, and I walked to the stall. I pushed the door and it swung open.

The hallway was thinning out. Everybody was on the way to their next class.

"I'll see you at lunch."

"OK."

Reed ducked into his typing class. The hallway was almost deserted, and coming toward me were two agents in suits. It was the tall gangly agent and Burden. Burden mumbled something under his breath but I couldn't make out what he said. He walked right past me, nodding politely as if he were just being neighborly.

30

W E HARDLY SAW THE FBI agents, but we all knew they were in the gymnasium. They didn't want to scare anybody. They were talking to everybody, everybody who knew Ian or had seen him that night. They started with all of the kids at the party and then they began questioning the rest of the students.

Me and Reed were the only two who didn't get questioned. They already knew what we were going to say.

At lunch, when I was on my way to the cafeteria, Ulster pulled me into his office and sat me down. "We need to talk," he said. "I don't know what's going on with you. I don't know if you have something to tell me. If you need to talk to me off the record, that's fine, I just want you to know that I'm here for you."

"OK." I was staring at the pictures of his two boys. His

oldest son, Robert, went to Carmen High, but he wasn't on the football team, he was this solemn introvert who played the xylophone in the school band.

Ulster shifted uncomfortably in his chair as if he were trying to scratch some part of his back that he couldn't reach. He continued, "Look, I just need you to know that this game on Saturday, well, it's not just a game for me. I don't much talk about this, but I have a personal stake in winning against Vegas. Me and . . . well, you know their Coach Ruben, anyway we have some history together and . . . well, it would be so sweet if we could finally crush those bastards."

I was standing in line in the cafeteria getting my food, meatloaf and mashed potatoes with vegetables. Through the glass partition I could see Lenore sitting with Amy at a table in the corner. I'd been thinking about it all morning, who I would sit with. I was planning to sit with Reed but I couldn't see him anywhere. I knew that if I didn't sit with the team it would appear suspicious. I needed them to know that nothing was the matter with me. I'd been feeling the stares all morning, but whenever I faced them they turned away.

I was walking into the dining area and trying to decide where to sit. I saw Mary but pretended that I didn't and just kept walking toward the football table. I sat down and it got quiet, as if they'd all been talking about something and now they couldn't.

D. J. Farby sat on my right.

"Hey."

"Hey."

And then he turned back to his food. We all ate in silence. I didn't want to look at Mary — I didn't know what she'd heard from the other students. I looked up and she was smiling back at me, sitting with Paula and Judy, and then she stood up with her tray and walked over to our table.

"Can I sit?"

"Sure."

All the guys turned their heads away as she sat down next to me — nobody was going to tell her that she couldn't. We all sat there, like Mrs. Aemes, in confusion, waiting for somebody to tell us what to do. And Mary felt like it was her fault. She was new to the table and so she took the silence personally.

"Should I leave?"

"No. It's OK," I said. We sat there eating quietly, and then she put her fork down and rested her head on my shoulder.

I glanced around the room and I noticed Kevin Bottoms sitting with some other boys. I watched him for a moment and wondered what he had said to the FBI. And then I saw the boy that he was sitting next to — Joe Maine, our waterboy. And suddenly I remembered my father pulling up to the school on Monday morning and Joe trudging across the parking lot with his bucket of orange wedges. I remembered how Joe had waved at me while I sat in the front seat of my father's car — wearing my hat.

Mary had her hand on my leg and was moving it up and

down. From the corner of my eye I could see Lenore walking out of the cafeteria with Amy.

"I have to go."

"Can I come with you?"

"No. I . . . I . . . gotta go."

And I got up and walked out of the cafeteria. I walked down the hall and then ducked into the bathroom. I was staring at myself in the mirror when I saw Reed's red Pumas under a stall door.

"Reed?" He opened the door. He was sitting on the toilet eating his lunch and looking miserable. "Are you all right?"

"I don't think I can do this."

I didn't know what to say. "Do you want to go outside and talk about it?"

"No." He shook his head. "I just want to be alone."

I went outside and walked around the back of the school to see if maybe those same kids were smoking in the alcove again, but there was just this guy and girl groping each other and so I kept walking. I crossed the street and headed over to the mall. I didn't want to go back to class — I didn't want to see anybody I knew ever again.

The mall had been around for years and was beginning to fall apart. It was full of those faces that you'd seen before, those invisible graduates, the ones who made you go *Yeah, I wondered what'd happened to them.* They rented out some shit trap in someone's basement and disappeared into the mall.

I stopped at the pet store. There was a row of dogs sitting in cages and as I got near them they became very excited, wagging their tails and trying to lick my hand. A sign above the cages read:

NO GUARANTEES OR EXCHANGES
SOLD AS IS

I asked the man at the counter if I could feed them but he told me that they'd already been fed for the day.

I didn't want to go back to Russell's class but I had nowhere else to go. I crossed the street and saw Brian again. He was leaning against the same truck and chatting with one of the older men. This time he saw me. I knew he saw me, but he didn't acknowledge it, he just casually turned back to the man he was talking to. For a second I wanted to start screaming at him right there in the middle of the road. I wanted to tell him that I knew he'd seen me, but instead I just crossed the street and went back inside the school.

31

I WALKED INTO Russell's class late. He didn't say anything as I went to my seat. I could feel the stares. I sat there wondering if they knew — everyone who'd been at Fred's party, everyone who'd seen the condition I'd been in that night.

From the window I could see all of the agents walking out to their cars. Burden was shaking their hands and patting them on the back. They stood around talking for a while and then they just got into their cars and drove off, all of them except for Burden and his gangly partner. They stood in the parking lot talking with each other and then Burden casually turned his head and stared right up into the second-story window, right into my eyes, as if he were saying, I know where you are and I know what you're doing. He stared right through me and then the two men walked back into the school.

*   *   *

As I was walking out of class, Russell stopped me.

"Could I speak with you?"

"Yeah."

"I saw your test yesterday. Is something going on?"

"I just . . . my mind was in a fog yesterday." I wasn't about to spill my guts to Russell.

"You think I don't see what you do?"

"Pardon me?"

"You may not be aware of this but I see what happens in this class." He looked distracted as he spoke, as if his heart weren't in it, as if he didn't really give a shit whether I was aware of it or not. "It's not my job to police the students, it's my job to teach math to anyone who wants to learn. You don't have to be here if you don't want to be. Are you aware that you have a choice?"

"Yes."

It was the first time that Russell had ever spoken to me, I mean actually ever shown any kind of concern. Everything that I had ever done flooded back into my head and I suddenly realized that Russell wasn't afraid of us — he was furious with us. All he wanted to do was teach. He just wanted to do his job and go home and be with his family.

"You're an intelligent young man and I don't say this to alarm you but I see you throwing your life away. I see you doing things that are only going to make your life more difficult." We stood there for a minute and I waited for him to continue. I don't know what I was waiting for, I guess I was waiting for him to give me some sort of solution, some idea of how I could make my life less difficult. But he didn't. He was finished. I see you throwing your life away.

32

W E WERE SITTING in the locker room getting
ready for practice. There was none of the regular
yelling and screaming; some of the guys were trying to act
like nothing was the matter but I could practically hear
what they weren't saying. I kept glancing at Joe Maine, who
was organizing the team's water equipment.

Reed sat by himself looking stricken, his head bent
down, lacing and unlacing his cleats. I turned to Fred, sitting next to me. "That was good hitting this morning."

"Thanks," he said coldly as he pulled his jersey over his
head. He wasn't himself. Nobody was.

Ulster walked in and gave us his pitch. "We've had some
interruptions this week" — he was calling Ian an interrup-
tion — "but I want you to put all this FBI business out of
your heads and I want to see us really play like a team to-

day." And then he had us gather together in a huddle and do our stupid school cheer.

We were storming out of the locker room into the hallway when I practically smashed right into Burden and his partner. His partner was holding a binder while Burden asked us our names, but when they came to me Burden didn't say a word, just waved me past. As I walked out the door I was hit by this brittle desert heat that singed my throat — I took a final glance back to see if they had stopped Joe, but he was still in the locker room. We sounded like a pack of horses, all forty of us clattering across the parking lot to the field in our cleats. I usually loved that noise, like a posse galloping together, but I didn't care about the noise that day, I just kept turning back to see if Joe would emerge from the school.

Some of our fathers were standing at the entrance to the bleachers. They were laughing at Benny's father, Ed, this manic wiseguy who was telling the story about how his wife had left him. We'd heard it a million times. She left him for some air-conditioning salesman from Phoenix who she met one night in the lobby of the Tropicana while Ed was at the slot machines. He found her at the bar with *Ken* two hours later and she had already decided that she was in love and was moving to Phoenix the following day.

"Two hours." He kept repeating. "Two hours." All of our fathers were laughing but the Penguin's father, Pete, was laughing the hardest, holding his guts and nearly sobbing while Ed animatedly told about how he'd tried to fight Ken and how the guy had knocked him out with one punch. Pete was laughing so hard that you couldn't help but wonder just what kind of pain he was in.

Ed's wife had been living in Phoenix with Ken for almost five years, "and the punch line is, I talked with her this morning and she told me — get this — she's never been happier in her life!"

Well, that did it, Peter Nutt's knees buckled and he was on the ground on his back screaming, "Two hours . . . two hours," while the players stepped over him on their way down the steps to the field.

My father was standing next to Stokely, who had pulled up in his cruiser, still in his uniform, to watch us practice. My father turned to me and smacked me on the back while Ed kept rambling.

"I got us two tickets to Neil Diamond tonight."

"Oh." That was all I could say. I didn't want to see Neil Diamond. I didn't want to go to Las Vegas with my father.

"We're gonna have some fun."

I knew why we were going to Vegas. Kimmy was gone and he needed to find a new girlfriend. For him it was like going into town to pick up supplies. He just wanted me along so that he wouldn't be alone. I kept watching the door to the school while my father talked to me. And then it opened and Fred stepped out carrying the team's water equipment and I knew that they were talking to Joe.

33

ALL I COULD SEE was colors rushing toward me. We were playing a scrimmage in preparation for the game against Las Vegas High on Saturday. I faded left, then pumped the ball hard through an opening between Benny and the Penguin. It hurtled like a bullet across the field toward Reed — he was rushing forward and then he turned and in that split second the ball flew right into his hands.

"I want you all at three-quarters strength, I don't want any of my boys getting hurt today." Ulster was on the side-lines chewing his sunflower seeds. I kept watching the front doors of the school, waiting for them to open and for the FBI agents to come outside. I wondered what Joe was telling them; I wondered if he remembered seeing me that morning.

Ulster was yelling instructions at us from the sidelines.

"That's not the way you shift! One, two, three, come on now!" But nobody cared, nobody felt like playing, I could feel them all staring at me now, wondering what I was hiding.

Fred snapped me the ball. I took a step back and glanced up at the doors to the school when suddenly from out of nowhere the Penguin smashed into me, swatting at the ball. I got up with my head spinning. "What was that for?"

The Penguin just shrugged and sauntered away like it was no big deal, like he just didn't know his own strength. And then out of the corner of my eye I saw Norman Lime standing at the top of the steps, jabbering into his cell phone. He lurched down the steps and over to Ulster and then cupped a hand over his eyes and began studying us on the field.

We went into a huddle.

"What the fuck is going on?" It was Travis Earl. He looked disoriented. This was his first year. He was supposed to block the Penguin but he wasn't expecting such force.

"Lime," someone explained.

And that was when things changed. We were supposed to be playing at three-quarters but now with Lime on the sidelines they all started hitting with everything they had. I glanced into the stands and saw that all of our fathers had stopped talking and were now sitting forward on their benches. Stubby was looking at me apprehensively like I held his future in my hands.

Fred snapped me the ball. I dropped back and hit Reed on a sideline fly pattern for seventeen yards before Ernie Gates flew at his knees and brought him down like a bucket of lead. Ulster was yelling at me from the sidelines. "Anybody else on that team of yours, Garvin?"

We went into a huddle.

"OK, we're going to do a thirty-two Y flat." I kept my eyes on the ground.

"How 'bout sharing the wealth, Garvin?" It was Stubby. He was wearing the same look on his face that he'd had the night he attacked me, real calm and ready to explode. Reed just stared at the ground, not saying a word.

"Just do what I tell you."

"C'mon, guys, let's just play."

"Fuck you."

"We do what Ulster tells us, asshole."

"What did you call me?"

"Asshole, asshole."

I glanced up and watched a couple of students coming out of the school.

"Why do you keep watching the front doors?"

I ignored Stubby and we took our positions. Fred snapped me the ball. Stubby and Reed were running a pattern where they both sprinted out, then cut hard to the inside and straight up the middle. The colors were rushing at me. I didn't see faces, they were only a distraction; I watched their hips. The rest of their bodies could be going one way but like Ulster said, "Your center of gravity never lies, it'll always give you away."

I could hear the jet planes from the Air Force base flying overhead. I thought about how perfectly they flew in formation and how we were just doing the same thing, practicing our simple maneuvers. We were all at war, whether it was in the air or on the field or just in some goddamn cafeteria in some little high school in the middle of fucking *it don't matter anyway!* But it did matter! Stubby and Reed were both heading into the end zone when suddenly I was seized by this dread. For some stupid reason I felt this crazy goddamn responsibility. I could hear this voice screaming at me that I had responsibilities and that there were consequences for my actions. This voice — it was so sure, like a rock, unwavering — was telling me that every choice was important, whether I said hello to the janitor or called some kid Snot or how I treated the pimply-faced freshmen smoking cigarettes in the alcove. I don't know why I was thinking about that but suddenly it just seemed like the most important thing in the world.

Reed and Stubby were charging toward the end zone and I could hear Ulster in my right ear screaming at me now, screaming at me to throw the ball. Reed was looking over his right shoulder, moving fast and just getting further away. I hated my father for making me play. I hated Lime for making me lie and Reed for trusting me and the team for counting on me and Burden for not giving up. I hated everybody for expecting me to be somebody I wasn't, someone who deep down I wasn't even sure existed.

My arm was moving back by itself now and I looked into the sky and I felt like I was soaring, like something was lifting me up and these thick dark clouds were floating past, floating right through me, and they were all in the shape of Fred's mother's sandwiches and I felt the ball being ripped from my hands and I didn't know if I had thrown it or if I had been tackled or even if I was alive anymore until nothing mattered anymore and I didn't care who caught the ball because all I wanted to do was sleep for a million years and then it all went dark and I was alone inside this warm wet cloud grinning and floating like one mad shimmering sandwich.

34

I WAS LYING on the ground with a heap of guys on top of me. There was this long silence and then everybody just started going crazy. I turned my head to the side and saw Ulster with his hand over his mouth and this blank look of astonishment. I heard the Penguin whisper, "Jesus Presley," as he watched the action downfield.

He was watching Reed catch the ball.

Downfield, Reed had already started walking back with the ball. Stubby joined him and put his arm across his shoulders, congratulating him. Reed nodded and just kept walking — he was looking directly at me. Other players walked up to him but Reed didn't acknowledge them and they just fell away. As Reed walked toward me I looked into his eyes and I saw pain. He was playing hurt. He was playing with more pain than he'd ever played with before. We shared a secret now. He hadn't asked for it, he was innocent, but I was taking that innocence away from him. He handed me the ball, and we were standing a foot away from each other when he nodded his head and said, "OK."

And then the doors to the school opened and Joe Maine stepped out with the agents. Burden and his partner were moving swiftly across the parking lot to the field. I turned and saw my father at the top of the bleachers, standing a head above everyone else and grinning stupidly, applauding my arm with those giant hands that had secrets of their own. His lips were moving but I couldn't make out what he was saying. He looked like a grinning phantom, some wild cowboy apparition. I stood there in the middle of the field staring up at my father and I saw what I was to become.

35

BURDEN AND HIS gangly partner swaggered down
the steps and over to Ulster. Burden spoke something
into Ulster's ear.

"Garvin. Banks." Ulster was waving us in and that was
when my father began jogging down the steps.

I walked across the field with Reed, our feet hitting the
ground in unison. Norman Lime wanted to speak to us but
Burden waved him away.

"We'd like to ask you boys a few questions," said Burden's partner.

My father was already standing between us. He pointed
at Burden. "He already talked to my son yesterday."

"Sheriff, this is now a federal investigation. We have reason to believe that Ian Curtis's disappearance is a possible
abduction or kidnapping."

"Oh, really? And what reason is that?"

"That's not something we can discuss."

"But you have evidence."

"That's classified."

He was lying. It was the only way the feds could get involved, by pretending they were investigating a kidnapping.

"My name is Pile." The gangly agent was wearing a dark-blue suit and a gray tie with a crisp white shirt. He extended his arm and shook my father's hand.

"How nice for you," said my father.

"Why don't we do this in the gymnasium?"

My father just stared at them both.

"Or we can do it in front of a grand jury," said Burden.

"He's not coming," my father said to Pile, pointing at Burden.

Pile was smiling. "Don't worry, I'll be asking all the questions. We're very intent on finding this boy. We don't want to interfere with your investigation and if there's anything we can do to help you, I want you please to let us know."

"You can tell me why you suspect it's a kidnapping."

Pile ignored this and kept on smiling as if my father hadn't said a thing. Reed just stood there, staring at the ground.

My father studied some imaginary dirt under his fingernails, then said, "OK, let's go."

"We'd prefer to speak to Neil alone."

"Well then, just consider me his legal counsel."

Stokely had wandered over from the stands. "Everything all right?"

"They want to ask the boys a couple of questions."

"Oh."

"Why don't you come with us," my father said to Stokely while smiling at Pile. Stokely joined us as we climbed the stairs past all the staring faces, then walked through the parking lot and into the school. Nobody was speaking as we walked down the hall to the gymnasium. I walked beside Reed, our cleats clacking loudly against the concrete floor.

Burden and Pile led us into the gymnasium. They had tables set up with a couple of chairs on either side, and some newspapers were taped over the little windows on the doors. Me and Reed sat down together across from Burden and Pile while my father sat alone at the side of the table and Stokely remained standing.

Pile began speaking. "You were both at Fred Billings's party Sunday night?" He said it as if he and Fred went way back.

We nodded our heads yes.

He turned to me. "What time did you leave the party?"

"It was after midnight."

"Did you see anybody on the road?"

"No."

"Did you stop anywhere on the road?"

"No."

"Had you been drinking?"

"Whoa, wait a minute," said my father.

"Your son is a suspect, Sheriff. We want to determine what his mental state was that night."

It didn't matter. Everybody knew I'd been drunk. "Yeah."

"How much did you have to drink?"

"I guess around seven beers."

Pile turned to Reed. "And what about you, were you drinking?"

"Yes, sir."

"What time did you leave the party?"

"It was after midnight."

"Any specific reason that you left?"

"I had Neil's hat and I was going to return it to him."

Reed knew they were going to ask him about this and so he was beating them to it.

"And did you?"

He didn't even pause — he surprised me with how quickly it came out. "No."

"How long was it after Neil left the party that you left?"

"I don't know."

"Approximately."

"Maybe ten minutes."

"Why didn't you bring the hat to his house?"

I could feel my father's eyes on Reed, watching him intently.

"It was late. I guess I didn't want to wake anybody up."

"Did you see anyone on the road?"

"No, sir."

"You didn't see a couple of kids walking along the side of the road?"

"No, sir."

"OK." Pile calmly rested one elbow on the table and his

whole body relaxed. He looked right into Reed's eyes. "When did you return Neil's hat to him?"

"It was after practice on Monday morning."

"Hmmm."

Reed nodded, trying to maintain eye contact with Pile. "You're sure about that?"

"Yes, sir."

I could feel the whole gymnasium slowly beginning to rock, like I was on a ship. And then Pile turned to me.

"Is that when he gave you your hat, Neil?"

I was about to say yes, I was about to agree with Reed, when my father spoke.

"Actually, if you don't mind my cutting in here, I remember Neil wearing his hat when he came home that night." My father said this very casually, like he was at a picnic. And then I remembered that he'd seen Joe Maine that Monday morning when we pulled up in the car — he knew that Joe had seen me wearing my hat and he had just seen Pile coming out of the school with him. My father knew they were trying to catch me in a lie.

"Why don't you just tell them the truth, son?"

I looked at my father. Reed was hugging his helmet and staring at the floor. My mind was racing as I tried to think of a story, but I couldn't, I was too nervous. And so I whispered to Pile, "Yes."

"Pardon me?"

"He gave me my hat on the road."

Pile and Burden glanced quickly at each other and then Pile continued.

"And how do you think he was able to catch up to you?"

I looked at my father.

"Why are you looking at your father?"

"Hey, give him a break, you're scaring him," my father growled.

"I don't know," I said.

"You don't know why you're looking —"

"I don't know how he caught up to me." I couldn't look at anything, not Reed, not my father or the agents. I just stared at the table in front of me.

"That's a five-mile stretch. How long does it take for you to get home from Fred's house?

"I don't know."

"Six minutes? Maybe seven?"

"I guess."

"And he left ten minutes after you? How could he possibly have caught up to you?"

"I don't know."

"You have no idea?"

"How bad is your hearing? That's what he just said." My father was getting impatient.

"I guess I was driving slow."

"Is it possible that maybe you stopped somewhere on the road?"

I wanted to tell them yes, that I had stopped on the road and that was how Reed had caught up to me, but my father said, "He's already answered that question."

Pile cleared his throat and composed himself.

"Tell me how you think Reed was able to catch up to you."

"You're doing it again."

"Oh, cut the bullshit," shouted Pile, losing it now. "Just tell us what fucking happened, all right! We have an eyewitness who says he saw Neil wearing his hat Monday morning. Reed caught up to him on a five-mile stretch, but Neil didn't stop on the road. There are ten minutes missing from your story, boy. You got ten good minutes missing."

Reed was squeezing his helmet and crying.

"That's it, we're done." My father stood up and grabbed my hand.

"Whoa, whoa, whoa, now just hold on a second." Pile was smiling. "OK, OK, I'm sorry." He forced a laugh. "Let's just take a breather, all right?"

"No, we're not going to take any goddamn breather. And you are not going to harass this young man just because he happens to be the son of a sheriff!"

"Pardon me?" said Pile.

Stokely was watching all of this in stunned amazement.

"You fuckin' feds got a hard-on for every cop you run into and you'd just love to pin this on some innocent kid because he's the sheriff's son! Now how 'bout I ask a couple of questions?" He turned to Reed. "How fast were you driving — pretty fast?"

Reed nodded.

"Ninety? Maybe a hundred?" Reed was starting to shake. "I've seen you drive that thing," my father said.

The room was still. Stokely stood behind everyone else, just watching, bewildered, not understanding what was going on.

"This is an FBI interrogation," said Pile.

"I think we're all after the same thing here, aren't we?" said my father.

"I doubt it," grunted Pile.

"If you don't have any more questions then why don't you just get the hell out of here?"

"We want to see your car," blurted Pile.

My father glared at Pile and then he smiled. "Get a warrant."

Burden took Pile by the arm, pulled him off to the side, and began whispering something in his ear. Finally Pile turned back to us. "OK." He was smiling. "OK. Apparently I have a temper. Well, I'm sorry this got so . . . awkward. We're going to leave now. And . . . we're just going to take Reed downtown to ask him a few more questions."

"Like hell you are."

"Like hell we aren't."

"You better show me some jurisdiction." My father stood up and his chair fell backwards. "There is no violation of federal law here, this is a local matter."

"Don't push me," said Pile, getting up in my father's face.

I watched Stokely's feet come apart like he was ready to fight. My father didn't back down from Pile but he didn't get angry either. He just gazed right through him and was practically grinning when he said, "Normally I'd let you take him away but there's just one small problem."

"And what's that?"

"He's under arrest."

"For what?"

Reed was staring at the floor. I wanted to say something, to apologize. My father said it without missing a beat. "Kidnapping."

"Kidnapping? There's no evidence!" shouted Burden.

"Oh," said my father. "Then why are you here?"

Burden was staring at my father with fury.

"Now get out of my county or I'll have you both arrested." They stood there for a moment. My father turned to Stokely. "Go ahead and cuff him."

"For kidnapping?" asked Stokely, looking bewildered.

"Suspicion of murder," my father muttered. "He was drunk. He was speeding. His story is all over the place."

Stokely pulled out his handcuffs and began telling Reed his rights. Burden and Pile stood there watching all of this and then finally they just stalked out of the room. Reed stood crying with his hands behind his back. My father looked at him and then turned away. Reed was trying to look at me but I couldn't face him.

Stokely guided Reed out with his right hand while carrying the helmet in his left. I stood there with my father. The room was empty and cold.

"So . . ." He was gazing down the length of the gymnasium. He looked like he was remembering something from a long time ago and I wondered what it was. He turned to me and smiled. "Are you ready to go to Vegas?"

36

LIKE I SAID, my father always took at least an hour to get ready for Neil Diamond. I could hear him downstairs in the bathroom, with Neil Diamond blasting from the stereo — he was listening to *On the Way to the Sky*. I just sat on my bed and thought about Reed. He was sitting in jail. My friend. I listened to my father turn the shower tap off and I felt rage. Every noise that came from downstairs filled me with rage. I hated him. And I hated that I was so afraid of him, so afraid of everything.

I walked downstairs. Some of the furniture was gone from the living room. I looked at the television screen — there was a hole right through the middle of it. Kimmy had spent the day clearing her stuff out. My father hadn't mentioned that she was gone, there was no note — it was as if she'd never even lived there.

His bedroom door was open. I could see him standing in front of his mirror, shaving with his electric razor. He saw me in the mirror and grinned. He was dressed all in black. He wore his black cowboy shirt with the purple piping, a black sports jacket, and black jeans. He'd bought brand-new lizard boots that day and his hair was oiled straight back. The streaks of silver in his hair were far more notice-able when his hair was greased. And he stank of cologne, like he was hiding some smell that he could never get rid of, like he was ashamed of his true smell.

"I'm not going to Vegas with you," I said.

He turned off his razor. "What was that?"

The sudden quiet scared me and for a second I lost my voice. "Uh . . ."

He winked at me. "Coupla quick minutes. Hey, why don't you wear your snakeskins?"

I went back upstairs, pulled off my dress shoes, and put on the snakeskin boots that my father had given me for my last birthday.

I listened to him downstairs. He couldn't stop moving. He was snapping his fingers and whistling and making clucking noises with his tongue. He kept moving around the house as he did his little tasks, putting on his bolo tie, shutting off the lights in the living room, readjusting the volume on the stereo. He always kept the music on until the last minute. As soon as he was ready to leave he would turn off the stereo and march out the door. He got very irritated if you asked him to do something after he'd turned off the music. One time when I was a kid, on our way out the door I'd asked him to tie my shoelaces and he'd yelled at me, "Why didn't you say something before I turned off the music!" I'd quickly learned that once the music was off it was time to get the hell out of the house.

37

THE SUN WAS SETTING as we left for Las Vegas. It set quickly in the desert. It always reminded me of how fast we were moving when sometimes it felt like we weren't moving at all. I hated Las Vegas. I wondered sometimes if I hated it just because my father liked it so much, but I think I hated it because of the way it made people behave. It made them desperate. It made them forget who they really were. They came to experience instant gratification and left with their lives in ruins. From far off, Las Vegas looked like fun, a magical city beckoning everyone with the promise of hidden treasures, but before you knew it you were inside of it and it was devouring you. It was constant noise and flashing lights and it made you feel like you were being assaulted.

We passed the Silverado Mobile Home Park where Dayton and Clyde both lived. There were a couple of Mexicans sitting on a bench waiting for a bus with their bottles of beer in paper bags. We drove in from the north end of town. The north side of Vegas was run-down and dangerous. It was all pawnshops, triple-X bookstores, bail bondsmen, wedding chapels, and a courthouse that was open twenty-four hours a day on weekends. We passed a store that was named simply WE BUY GOLD. The American Burial and Cremation Services claimed "Dignified Services at Affordable Prices." An old, leathery-faced drunk staggered in front of our car glaring at us as he made his way to a filthy motel that boasted ELVIS SLEPT HERE.

We passed a billboard that read Free Million-Dollar Slot Pull at Ballys! All the billboards in Vegas promised instant fortunes. They said things like FIVE MILLION PAID OUT DAILY or showed a picture of someone who had just struck it rich at the slot machines. On the way out of town all the billboards advertised attorneys, storage space, and ninety-five-cent breakfasts.

As we drove up the strip, my father could barely contain his glee. It was as if all his problems had dissolved as he entered the city limits and all that lay ahead was rapture. We pulled into the MGM Grand and left the car with the valet. My father gave him a ten-dollar tip and strode to the front doors with me trailing behind him. We walked into the lobby, which was decorated with touches from *The Wizard of Oz*. In the center of the lobby was Dorothy with the Scarecrow, the Tin Man, and the Cowardly Lion, all skipping together down the yellow brick road. My father stopped in the middle of the lobby and let everyone admire him in his new boots while he muttered something about the hotel design's being so "faithful to the original."

"I'm going to play some twenty-one," he said as I followed him to one of the gaming tables. Because I wasn't of legal age, I just watched. He bought a hundred dollars' worth of chips. He put down twenty dollars and lost it. A waitress came along and took his order: Midori on the rocks with a twist of lime. "Thank you, Ellen," he said, eyeing her name-tag. As she walked away my father looked at the dealer and whistled under his breath. Ellen was young and pretty with a terrific body and large fake breasts. Every woman who worked in Vegas had fake breasts. Even Bernice had fake breasts, and she worked in a ticket booth. My father had told me that men tipped the waitresses in direct proportion to their chest size. Not him, he tipped everybody well, he was only cheap with himself. He'd told me about one wait-ress who had gotten fired because some doctor gave her im-plants so enormous that the management considered them obscene. She refused to have them removed and so they put her to work in the laundry. After a while she got bored and so she changed her name to Aphrodite and took a job strip-ping at the Olympic Gardens, where my father told me she "made obscenely large tips to equal her monstrous boobs."

My father lost five straight hands. Ellen came back with his drink just as he was losing his final hand. We wandered over to the ticket counter. Bernice was working at the win-dow. Her face brightened when she saw us.

"Hey, gorgeous, how's tricks?" he said to her. Bernice giggled and fixed her hair.

"I'm doing good, baby," she said. "They just switched my schedule so this is my Friday." In Vegas all the employees are on different schedules and so the last day before their work week ends they refer to as their Friday. I never got used to hearing grown-ups calling some random day their Friday. It sounded like the way three-year-olds would talk if they had jobs. Bernice pushed the envelope with the tickets toward my father. It read:

> Garvin — Two tickets for Neil Diamond to the
> two most handsome men in Nevada.
>
> Love Berny

I stared at Bernice's handwriting. Her *t*s were crossed through the middle and I noticed the way she wrote the *y* at the end of her name: it flew away and nearly traveled right off the paper. The floor fell out from under me and I felt like I was falling.

"How are you, darling?"

"I'm OK," I said to her, the room still spinning. She was looking at me with her brittle hair and her big fake white teeth, and she looked like a devil. A few years ago, her teeth had gone rotten and then, overnight, she had a brand-new set of perfect white teeth.

"You just get more handsome every time I see you." I could smell the decay in her mouth as she spoke to me. I told my father that I needed to use the bathroom.

I stood at the sink waiting to throw up, but I couldn't. I stared at myself in the mirror. I was shaking. My body was vibrating with rage. Bernice had written that letter from my mother. A man walked in and took a leak at the urinal. He turned on the tap beside me and started washing his hands. He was missing the tip of his pinkie finger. I looked at the man for a second and he walked out without drying his hands.

My insides felt like they were going to quit. I knew that I had to get away. I had to get away from my father, away from all the lies. One of my knees buckled and I fell to the floor. And then the door opened and two men were standing behind me. I watched them in the mirror; they looked familiar, with short-cropped hair, all business.

"Neil?"

I had seen them earlier that afternoon at school.

"What do you want?" I tried to stand but I couldn't.

"We want to help you."

"No you don't." The words just spilled out of me.

"We think we can help you."

"How are you going to help me?" I wished they hadn't seen me on the floor. I stood up and faced them. They were big; I could look them in the eyes, but they were much larger than me.

"We need you to tell us what happened. Don't worry, you're not going to get in trouble." This one agent was looking at me with a kindly smile and I knew he was lying. "You don't have to be afraid anymore."

His telling me that I didn't have to be afraid made me furious. I knew that Burden had told him about the sand in my father's living room. I wanted to tell them that they didn't know who I was, that they didn't know anything about me.

"Well, I don't want to talk to you."

"We don't have a lot of time. We want you to come with us."

"No." I moved to leave but one of the men took a step forward and grabbed me by the elbow. I pulled away. "Don't touch me!"

"We just want to —"

"No you don't. You're liars! You're all a bunch of liars!" They were both holding on to me and trying to cover my mouth. "Let go of me!" I was screaming at them.

"Shut the fuck up!" one of them hissed at me.

I tried to swing at him but they were holding me too tightly. And just then a man walked in and stood staring at us and the agents loosened their grips and I bolted out the door.

My father was still standing at the ticket booth talking with Bernice. As I walked toward them I turned back to see if the agents were following me, but they weren't, they were nowhere in sight.

38

NEIL DIAMOND was onstage singing "Love on the Rocks." My father was transfixed. He sat with his jaw wide open, cradling his Midori.

I couldn't stop thinking about the letter. My father had told me once that my mother had just picked up one day and left. He'd come home and she was gone. He told me that she hadn't cared much for Carmen and hadn't wanted to spend the rest of her life in a small town. But she hadn't written that letter; Bernice had. What had really happened with my mother?

We were all standing as Neil Diamond, his satin shirt drenched with sweat, took his bows. As we filed out of the theater, my father said, "Let's go meet him." In the past, my father had scorned all the celebrity hounds who hung around the stage door after the show. It upset him that they couldn't just enjoy the show and allow Neil Diamond his privacy.

We stood by the stage door with a crowd of other people. My father held his program loosely in his left hand and a fresh Midori in his right. He kept saying, "What a show, what a show. Every time I see him, he gets better."

There was this loud, swollen-looking man in a cowboy hat who was with a pretty young girl who couldn't stop glancing at her pager. My father was cracking some jokes that he'd heard on television.

"What do you call an empty bottle of Aqua-Velva on the side of the road?" he asked the cowboy.

The cowboy started roaring with laughter. "I don't know for sure."

"An Indian artifact," said my father. This got a big laugh from the crowd. "And what do you call a half-empty bottle of Aqua-Velva on the side of the road?" They all shook their heads. "Well, that one's a *rare* Indian artifact," he announced. The cowboy was holding his ribs. He was laughing so hard that no sound was coming out. Even his escort started laughing a little bit.

"So, is this your daughter?" my father asked the cowboy. The cowboy stopped laughing and suddenly everyone became uncomfortable. My father tossed back the rest of his Midori. "Anyone who pays for sex is scum in my book." I'd never heard my father speak to a stranger that way before. He was always charming and cordial to everyone else, reserving his temper for when he got home. The cowboy was about to say something but then my father gave him a look and the cowboy just deflated and shuffled away with his date. After that everyone turned away from my father and he just stood there looking awkward and ridiculous.

Neil Diamond emerged from the stage door and began signing autographs. Everyone surrounded him except for my father. He just stood there and watched. When Neil Diamond was finished he looked at my father but my father couldn't speak — he was frozen. Finally Neil Diamond smiled and nodded and gave my father a look that I'd never seen anyone give him before. He looked at my father with compassion. And then, flanked by hotel security, he walked to the exit and out to his limousine.

My father waited for Neil Diamond to disappear before he went over to the blackjack table. He lost another couple of hundred dollars and splashed a few more Midori into himself. He started getting pretty loud and he kept telling everyone that his son had the best throwing arm in the country. "My boy is going to be All-American," he told the dealer. The dealer smiled wearily at me. I kept looking around to see if we were being followed.

We left the car at the MGM Grand and took a taxi to the Olympic Gardens. I was too young to get in but when the doorman asked me for my I.D. my father pushed a hundred-dollar bill into his palm.

"Look at all this pussy," said my father.

There were four stages, with topless women dancing on each one. Against the walls women would dance personally for guys for twenty dollars a song. We sat down at a booth and my father ordered us a couple of drinks. He was nodding his head slowly and gazing around the room and then he stood up and mumbled to no one in particular that he was going to the bathroom. I was looking around to see if anyone looked suspicious but it was impossible to tell because everyone did.

A couple of strippers sat down beside me. I guess they were a team; they were wearing matching pink fluorescent bikinis with white hearts. Their names were Sandy and Briani.

"What's your name?"

"Neil."

"Where are you from, Neil?"

"Carmen."

"Let me tell you what we specialize in." Sandy reached her hand down between my legs and started rubbing me. "We specialize in anything goes." And then, with her other hand, she popped her tit out of her top and showed me her nipple. I looked over at her friend Briani, who was gazing around the room with a bored expression.

"You don't bite, do you?" Sandy asked.

"Pardon me?"

"Do you bite?"

"Well, I might nip a little."

She laughed as if I were the first guy who had ever said that. "So, you want a dance, or what?"

"Maybe later."

They both got up and walked to the next table.

I watched a beautiful woman dancing in front of some

man while he sat drunk and motionless, gazing intensely at her ace of spades. She wasn't actually dancing — she was gliding an inch above him and writhing like a panther. I'd never seen a woman move like that. There was something violent and animalistic about the way she bucked and rolled. It scared me, made me feel out of control. Some guy saw me watching and leaned over, "It's his dance, buddy, not yours." The way she was moving was hypnotic and I had to force myself to pull my eyes away; it was the most erotic thing I'd ever seen but for some reason it made me feel like I was watching something being murdered.

Every two minutes another girl would come to the table and I just started having the same conversation over and over again.

"Hi, what's your name?"

"Neil."

"How old are you, Neil?"

"Twenty-one."

"You don't look it."

"Thank you."

"You want a dance?"

My father came back from the bathroom and sat down. A young blond girl with full lips and a great body immediately sat down next to him. Her name was Angel. She was quiet and seductive; she looked right into my father's eyes and he suddenly got very quiet. This lady sat down beside me who had long black hair, dark chocolate eyes, and the largest breasts I'd ever seen in my life.

"Hi, what's your name?"

"I'm Neil."

"My name's Aphrodite." She smiled. "How would you like these big titties in your face, little sailor?" My father was grinning at me. We both got up with our strippers and walked over to the wall. We sat in the corner, separated by a transparent pole filled with water bubbles that kept changing color.

Aphrodite was standing with her back to me, wiggling her ass in my face, and so I watched my father. Angel stared into my father's eyes and moved slowly over him with her hips. He wore a blank look of surrender, like he was falling in love against his will. Stevie Nicks played on the sound system. She was singing about being a gypsy. Every song was costing my father forty dollars for the both of us, but he didn't care.

"Looks like your daddy's falling in love."

I watched him whisper into Angel's ear like he was confessing something. She nodded slowly and whispered something back to him. I started to think about Lenore, about the last time I'd seen her. I couldn't believe that it was just that afternoon, it seemed so long ago.

"I could make a lot more money spreading my legs for any Joe on the strip, but I'm a nice person."

"What?"

Aphrodite had her ass in my face and was talking to me from between her legs. "I'm a nice person. That's why I could never make money on my back. I'm just not that kind of person."

I was looking past Aphrodite when I saw Kimmy dancing

on one of the stages. She was wearing sunglasses and black leather boots up to her knees. My father was too engrossed in Angel to notice anything. When the song ended, Aphrodite asked me if I wanted another dance but I told her that I was fine and that my father would pay her.

My father didn't see Kimmy as we walked out of the bar. The room was so dark that it was difficult to assess the damage he had done to her face the night before. I guess stripping was the only job she could get where no one would notice how hurt she was.

It was muggy outside, the air thick and sharp like a storm was gathering. My father grabbed my shoulder from behind and spun me and suddenly he was hugging me, squeezing me tightly but not making a sound. And then he said, "I'm proud of you, I know I don't tell you that too much, but I am." He was looking into my eyes. "You deserve everything," he said to me. I wanted it to be true. I wanted it all to be OK. I wanted to believe him when he put his arms around me and told me that I deserved everything, but I knew he was drunk. I knew he would never remember that moment. He was a liar and I couldn't trust anything he said.

His eyes were welling up and he was muttering about how he could have done better. And I heard myself saying no, that he'd done the best he could. And yet I wanted to tell him that I hated him and that he deserved to fall away forever for what he'd done to me. But I couldn't. He was my father. And no matter where I went I was never going to escape him.

39

WE WERE WALKING up the Las Vegas strip, past
Caesar's and Ballys. He wanted to walk. He stopped
at the Holiday Inn to take a piss. It was two in the morning and there were still people dropping their hard-earned
money into slot machines, wishing things were different. At
the beginning of the night they'd started with hope. They'd
been sober then and they'd played with restraint, but by two
in the morning fear had set in and they were hurriedly trying to break even, just trying to get back to zero. I wondered
where Reed was and how he was doing.

I watched my father walk toward me from the bathroom.
Even drunk, his walk was precise and official. He stopped
and watched an old lady play a round of blackjack and con-
gratulated her when she won a five-dollar chip. She barely
noticed him as she sucked on her cigarette and motioned
for the dealer to hit her again.

"I'm hungry," he said to me.

We stopped at the New York, New York Hotel. The only restaurant open was Broadway Burger so my father ordered the Meadowlands Special, a foot-long hot dog with fries and a vanilla milkshake. He sat on a bench chewing his hot dog while I stood and watched him. I felt drunk and nervous and not like sitting down. Finally I told him I was going to piss and I wandered through the make-believe New York streets looking for a bathroom. When I came back, he was talking to some lady who looked to be around forty-five.

"I got a surprise for you." There was still mustard at the corner of his mouth.

She had one of those tans that come out of a bottle and that at three in the morning begin to give your face an orange hue. She gave me a thin, tired smile and said, "I hear you're looking for a date, sweetheart."

Her name was Gloria. We introduced ourselves to each other as we waited for my father to pay for the room. Nobody spoke as we took the elevator up to the eighth floor, but my father started to whistle. It was a song that Neil Diamond had sung earlier that evening, a single he'd released in the summer of '73 called "The Last Thing on My Mind."

In the room, Gloria asked my father if he minded her using the telephone to call her company and let them know where she was. I imagined some guy with a gun sitting in a car outside waiting for her. If she took too long he could come in blasting and there I'd be, naked and trembling.

My father was crouched over the minibar fighting with the key while I made small talk with Gloria. She was from

Denver, she told me. I wondered if she was lying but she didn't seem to care if I knew where she came from so I guessed that she wasn't.

"How long have you lived in Las Vegas?"

"Too long. So, how do you want to do this?"

"He's gonna fuck you, then I'm gonna fuck you," said my father as he opened the lock on the minibar.

She pulled her dress over her head. That was all she was wearing, a dress. It made me think of the race cars whose tires could be changed in just a few seconds because they were attached with only a single bolt. Gloria reminded me of a race car, built for speed. "Go ahead and take off your clothes," she said as she went into the bathroom.

My father was sitting on a chair staring at me with a drink in his hand as I got undressed. And then he stood up and announced to no one in particular, "I'm gonna get some ice." I took off the rest of my clothes while he went down the hall. I pulled back the covers and lay down on the bed. Gloria came out of the bathroom with a face cloth that she'd run under hot water. She laid the cloth between my legs and gently pulled it up toward my belly. As she dragged the hot cloth over me I felt myself stiffen.

"That's it," she said.

She had what must have been a caesarian scar just below her belly button. I'd never seen one before and it suddenly occurred to me why they were called caesarians and it seemed like an awful joke, naming the port of childbirth after some guy who'd gotten stabbed to death. I reached over and turned off the bedside lamp while she tore open a condom package with her teeth. The only light in the room was from the bulb at the doorway. My father walked in as she was beginning to stroke me. He was silent as he sat back down on his chair and plopped some ice cubes into his drink. I could feel his dead eyes watching us like we were television.

Gloria lay on her back, then took me in her hand and guided me in between her legs. I moved in and out slowly while she exhaled a soft, delicate sigh at each thrust. Gradually I bent my elbows and lay down on top of her so that my chest was touching her breasts, but she whispered through clenched teeth, "Don't touch me." I pushed myself up and stared at the painting of the Statue of Liberty above the bed. I glanced at my father sitting on his chair. His jeans were around his ankles; he had a drink in his left hand and was stroking himself with his right. He just sat there masturbating like we were light-years away from him and he was seeing for the first time something that had happened a million years ago. Gloria reached down and pulled me in deep and even as I was coming I felt no relief. Not even for a second. I felt like the people downstairs in the casino, just trying to get back to zero.

She went into the bathroom and I heard her turn on the faucet. My father continued masturbating. I don't think he even knew I was there anymore. I got dressed. "Let's go," I said. He nodded slowly but he didn't move. "C'mon, Dad." It was the first time I'd ever called my father Dad. It surprised me as I heard it come out of my mouth. I don't know why I called him that. Maybe I just wanted to get out of there as quickly as possible and I was trying to shock him, break through the fog of booze and confusion. But actually, and I know it's crazy, I think it was the first time that I ever really saw him. I gently shook his shoulder and said, "C'mon," then reached down and helped him pull his jeans back on.

Gloria came back out of the bathroom and told me, "Happy birthday." And that was when I realized that my father had told her it was my birthday. He wanted her to think that this was a special occasion. He didn't want her to think that we were just a couple of degenerates.

40

AS WE WALKED back to the MGM Grand my father seemed to have forgotten what had just happened. He chuckled to himself, "Aphrodite, atta girl," as if the Olympic Gardens was the last place we had been. He didn't have any money left to pay the valet so he stopped at an ATM. He'd given Gloria his last two hundred dollars — he got in a hassle with her over the bill and finally just gave her what she wanted, which was everything in his wallet. As he pushed in his card I was standing a few feet away and suddenly a group of people walked past me and I felt myself being pulled around the corner. It was the two FBI agents from earlier. They dragged me into a doorway and threw me hard against a wall. My head hit the concrete and it woke me up.

"All right, listen! You got two choices: you can talk to us

right now, right here, or you can wait until your friend gets out, because in less than seventy-two hours he's going to be released and he's going to tell us what you won't!"

"How do you know?" We all turned. It was my father. He was standing behind the agents, casually stuffing his money into his wallet.

"You can't hold him longer than three days without pressing charges," said one of the agents.

"Then we'll press charges."

"For what? What are you going to charge him with? You don't have a body!"

"Maybe one'll turn up." My father was just gazing back at them, almost expressionless. The agents were looking at my father and they had nothing to say. It was the first time I understood just how far my father was willing to go. "Now step away from my son."

We walked back to the MGM Grand and got the car from the valet. I climbed into the driver's seat and began to drive. The agents had just walked away from us. There was nothing they could do. I hadn't been driving for long before my father became irritated with me for stopping at a yellow light.

"C'mon, let's go," he yelled.

At the next set of lights I rolled a couple of feet past the white line and he screamed at me to get out of the car so that we could trade places. He drove us out of Vegas. We sped away, leaving the noise and the lights behind us. We headed north past the Olympic Gardens, past the sleazy motels and pawnshops and trailer parks. Las Vegas fell away behind us until all we faced was blackness.

And that was when my father turned off the headlights. We were hurtling through the darkness, he had his window down and Neil Diamond blasting from the stereo, and he was shrieking into the night. I wanted to scream at him, but I didn't. When he turned the lights back on we were on the wrong side of the road. He corrected the car and then killed the lights again and that was when I realized that there was no such thing as a mistake. Everything I had ever learned I'd learned from my father. Ian Curtis had not been an accident. I had been on a collision course with him for years.

"Stop the car!"

He hit the brakes without turning the headlights back on. It was dark and I couldn't see his face.

"Don't ever yell at me again," he said.

I was shaking. "What happened to my mother?"

"Some things," he said, "some things you don't need to know."

My father opened his door and got out of the car. I got out too and repeated my question. I couldn't see him, but I yelled out, "Don't run away from me!" He was right in front of me. I could feel him. "What did you do with him?"

My father grabbed me by the collar and pulled me toward him. I could feel his power. "Don't ask me questions, boy."

"Tell me! You tell me!"

"He's dead! Now just you forget about it!"

"Where is he?" I was screaming at him.

He held me against the car, pushing my face against the warm metal hood. "It's over," he said. And then he pushed me back inside the car.

We barreled down the road. A stray dog sauntered in front of the headlights. My father swerved, saving the stupid dog's life.

"Bernice wrote that letter to me."

My father didn't speak.

"When I was five. Didn't she?"

He just stared straight ahead, watching the road and listening to Neil Diamond. I hit the eject button on his CD player and yanked out his Neil Diamond CD. I threw it out the window, and now we were driving in silence. He just kept staring at the road.

I thought about the future. About playing college ball. I thought about Lenore and Reed and the janitor and the kids who gave me the cigarettes. And then I thought about Ian Curtis. He was waking me up at night, watching me from behind curtains and leering at me from passing cars. And no matter what I did, I could never bring him back. I imagined his parents sitting at home wondering where their son was. They would never stop searching. They would never have any peace. And then I thought about the letter that Bernice had written and I couldn't stop trembling.

"I know she wrote that letter."

"Well, aren't you clever," was all he said.

"Where is she? Where's my mother?"

"I don't know where she is."

He turned the radio on. I reached over and switched it off. He threw his hand across and caught me on the chin.

"You watch it, boy!"

"Where is she?" I screamed at him.

"I told you what I said," he roared. "I told you what I said!"

"I want the truth, goddamn you!"

He drove in silence. And I could feel myself fading away, fading further and further until I became the front of the car devouring the road underneath and there was nothing left of me but fear. And that was when I realized that it wasn't mine. This fear. It was his. I'd never thought of my father as being afraid of anything, but sitting beside him I realized that fear was all he was. And I had been carrying it my whole life. I could feel this strength growing inside of me, and I was grinning in the darkness, grinning because I knew that I didn't have to be afraid anymore. I didn't have to keep this secret anymore. It wasn't mine to keep.

41

H E DIDN'T SAY a word as we entered the house. I heard the bottle opening in the kitchen as I climbed the stairs to my room. As I entered my room I heard thunder roll up and over the house like a bulldozer. A few seconds later, the rain hit the house like bullets and the house began to shake. Lightning streaked across the sky, lighting up the desert. Animals looked up with surprise and bolted for the nearest rock.

I sat on my bed, gazing at my mother in the photograph, wondering if I would ever see her again. And then I walked back down the stairs. My father was staring at a gaping hole in the plastic. The rain and wind were whipping against him, soaking him. He took a long drink from the bottle in his hand. He turned and looked at me. I gasped. I barely recognized him anymore.

"Where is he?" was all I said.

*   *   *

My father walked in front of me, carrying a shovel over his right shoulder and a flashlight in his left hand. We didn't need the flashlight — the sky lit up the desert every few seconds, like it was playing chicken with the world.

We passed a fox that scurried over to a cactus and sat shivering, watching us, half of its coat torn off by some enemy.

We walked for half a mile until we came to a small grove of Joshua trees. My father stood there for a moment, then took four steps from the tree and drove the shovel into the ground. He tossed me the flashlight and started walking away.

I still don't know what made me tackle him. I had what I wanted — I had the body. I ran at him low and fast and he went down easily. I got on top of him and held him down with my knees, but I wasn't as strong as he was and he knocked me off. I got up and tried to get away but he came lunging at me. I ducked out of the way like he had taught me. It was a quick, barely perceptible shift of the body that took me out of the line of fire.

My father landed on the ground. As he got to his feet, the night sky lit up and we faced each other, circling each other. He had me in a headlock as he dragged me to the ground. His first punch broke my nose. I felt my face go numb in the darkness. As the sky lit up, I looked up from the ground and saw surprise on my father's face. The night turned black and I felt his boot in my ribs.

I staggered to the tree and pulled myself up. I saw him

running at me, but this time I moved and clipped his knees. He went down fast and I kicked him in his side. I tried to stomp his head, but he grabbed my foot and pulled my legs out from under me. My feet slid across the mud and we were wrestling on the ground.

And then he was strangling me. He was tightening on my throat and I was looking into his eyes and I saw that I wasn't looking at rage anymore. I was looking at fear. And behind all that fear, behind all those millions of miles of darkness, I saw this light. I saw it for the first time as my father tried to kill me.

It was love.

The bump above his right eye was bleeding and his mouth was cut open but he wasn't far away anymore, he was right in front of me, and he was real. I started to laugh. I felt like we could see each other for the first time and I didn't feel afraid — a hot, searing fire was knifing its way across my throat and I was laughing.

The sky lit up behind my father, a ferocious ball of crimson exploding, and then it went dark. I clutched at my throat, my body convulsing, and then it was light again and I wasn't looking at my father anymore.

I was looking at my mother.

She was reaching out for me, reaching out with her hands. And suddenly I could see her face, her jaw jutting out in front of her, teeth bared, eyes aflame, and in her hands, stretched tightly between two fists, were her pantyhose.

And she was strangling me. And I was screaming at her

to stop. No! Please! Please! But no sound was coming. I was three years old and I had scratched Mommy's dance record. Mommy was mad and I was begging for her to stop but she wouldn't. She couldn't. She hated me for killing her dreams. She hated me and she hated my father for making her stay and take care of me. And then I saw the gun. And I heard the single blast that changed all of our lives forever. I watched my mother fall limply to the ground in front of me. And that was when I knew what had happened. That was when I knew that my mother was not living with a dentist in a mansion in Beverly Hills and that I was never going to see her in a toothpaste commercial. That was when I knew that she was gone forever. And maybe I had always known it in my heart, but I hadn't wanted to listen to my heart. I'd just wanted everything to be OK.

My father had probably wondered for all those years if I remembered, if I was just keeping quiet for him, but he knew the instant that it came back to me. He saw it in my face. And he let me go.

42

I LAY ON THE GROUND bleeding and covered in mud. My father had walked back to the house and left me there. My ribs were broken, my face was twisted around, and the bones in my foot were crushed in a dozen places.

The rain fell on my face, washing the blood and the mud from my eyes, and it all came back to me. Those green drinks that she'd begun pouring first thing in the morning. Her green coffee, she'd called it — and her laugh, like a furious snarl from out of nowhere. That morning I'd sat and watched her doing her laundry and then, bored, I'd wandered into the living room and tried to put one of her dance records on the turntable. It was an accident. I didn't mean to do it. She shrieked as the needle scraped against the groove. I knew that I had done something wrong and so I ran behind the curtains to hide. And then the curtains flew away and she was standing in front of me and I was shaking and I wanted her to hug me and none of it made any sense. *I didn't mean to do it. I didn't mean to do it.* Those words. I'd been chanting them my whole life.

After a while, the rain stopped falling and a pink thread of light peeked out over the horizon. I lay there staring at the sky and listening to my breath. The screaming had stopped and there was no noise at all. For the first time in my life I could hear peace in the silence and I just wanted to lie there forever. I wanted to lie there and watch the sky change colors and I didn't want to fight anymore.

I thought about my father and the secret that he had kept for all those years. I gradually began to understand, like tiny sundrops over my body I began to see it all — the wall that he'd torn down, the wall where he'd killed her that was now just a plastic sheet flooded with sunlight, where we couldn't look without squinting. And his Midori — it was the only place he could find peace and maybe he thought he could visit her, meet up with her somewhere down at the bottom of the bottle. And the letter. He had asked Bernice to write to me because he'd wanted me to know that I was loved. Even if he couldn't tell me himself, he wanted me to know that Mommy loved me and Daddy did too.

43

I COULDN'T WALK back to the house. And so I crawled. I opened the front door and hobbled down the hall. I entered the living room covered in mud and saw my father sitting silently on his chair with his service revolver in his lap. He didn't look big to me anymore; I thought my father was a huge man but sitting there in his chair he looked broken and harmless and I wondered what I had ever been afraid of.

"I know what happened," I said to him. "I know that you killed her." He was looking right into my eyes when I told him, ". . . And I know that you saved my life." He didn't move, his face didn't flinch, but tears began rolling down his face.

"She loved you," he said. He kept repeating it through his tears. My father had never told me that he loved me, and I wondered right then if maybe it was because he hadn't wanted me to think that that was what love looked like. I always thought he was invulnerable. I don't know why I thought that anyone could ever be invulnerable. He had painted himself so tightly into a corner that there was no room for anyone else, and what he feared more than anything was being alone. "She was innocent." That was what he said. "I just wanted to save her. I wanted to make up for everything that had happened to her before." I took the gun away from him and emptied the bullets into my hand. He looked at me, his face still muddy, his eyes red and swollen. "Everything I did was what I thought was right."

Through the window I saw the police car moving slowly up the driveway. We sat there until Stokely and Quinlan rang the doorbell. My father had called them himself. He didn't want the FBI getting involved, he wanted his own men to get the credit for this. They let us get cleaned up and then took us down to the sheriff's office. My father was crying when he told them what had happened. He told them about Ian and about my mother. They seemed like they didn't want to be there, they just kept staring at the pad of paper that Quinlan was writing on. They didn't even speak, they just sat across the table shifting nervously while me and my father told them everything.

AFTER

44

I SPENT MOST of my waking hours being afraid of my father. Even when I tried to explain to myself that he was the sheriff of Carmen and that his job was to protect and serve, it didn't matter; I was the reason he had been abandoned, and he hated me for it. Maybe it wasn't logical, but nothing true is ever logical. I was afraid of my father because I didn't know what he was capable of. That was why I put Ian Curtis in the trunk. I didn't expect my father to find him. And I didn't expect him to hide him. When he saw Ian's body in the trunk it must have confirmed everything he'd feared. "Like father, like son," he'd said. His greatest fear was that I would become him. When he hid Ian's body it was the beginning of my questioning my father, it was the beginning of my questioning everything, and in the end it was the beginning of my understanding his reasons.

I'm serving two years for vehicular manslaughter and my

father is serving two years for aiding and abetting in the concealment of Ian's body. We are both serving time at a minimum-security prison near Boulder City, Nevada. There was no trial. I remember the Curtises staring at me during the arraignment. They didn't sit together. Mr. Curtis sat toward the back of the courtroom and Mrs. Curtis sat up front with Burden and Mary. I'd heard that they'd separated and that Mr. Curtis had moved into a condo in Vegas. I was afraid they would scream at me or begin weeping hysterically but they just sat and listened. If nobody told you, you wouldn't have known they were Ian's family. They appeared calm, but you can't really tell a thing about a person from just looking at them.

I didn't cry when I told the court my story, I just told the facts. I didn't tell the whole truth and nothing but the truth. I didn't tell about my fear. It may have been the truth but nobody really wants the whole truth. In the end the whole truth would take forever. I looked at Burden when I told my story. He knew more about me than anyone else in the courtroom. He had sat in my father's house.

Three weeks after I drove into Ian, the dream began. I was heading directly toward him, I could see the horror in his eyes, and as I twisted the wheel, the steering locked and I sent him soaring. They gave me a pill to help me sleep but the dream didn't go away. I still dream it most nights. I think that a part of me doesn't want it to go away — a part of me needs it, like there's some dark hallway in me that still needs to be reminded. And so all that's left is regret. And no matter how badly my heart wants it to be different, no matter how many times I try and turn the wheel away from him in my dream, he is dead. For as long as I live, Ian Curtis will be dead.

Sometimes the guilt feels so unbearable that I just want to join him. But then there are moments, these brief moments like a few weeks ago when Reed came to visit me, when it all goes away. And so now I live in moments. I didn't think Reed would ever want to see me again. But maybe that's why I'm in jail, because had it been different, had I been Reed, I know that I would never have visited. He was drafted by UNLV — Lime drafted him — and he's going to start playing in the fall. He sat there and told me about his plans. It's funny how you can see a person a certain way for so long and then one day you see him totally differently and he didn't do a thing to change.

Sometimes I think about how I'll go and see Reed play for his new school. I imagine myself watching him from the sidelines, screaming for him as he runs up the middle, leaping to my feet as he crosses into the end zone and the ball sails into his arms. Raising my fist when he turns to me, letting him know that I support him, letting him know that I love him.

The other morning, out in the yard, I watched my father playing basketball. He was far away but he saw me too and he walked to the fence. I don't know how long we stared at each other, maybe it was only a few seconds, but I could see that his distant look was gone. That look in his eye that I had spent my whole life wondering about, it was gone, and I was staring at a different part of my father. I lifted my hand and so did he. The part of my father that terrified me for so long had disappeared, just floated away with our secret. He looked like a little boy, standing behind the fence, his long arms dangling at his sides. I still have the photograph of the three of us. I used to cover up my father with my thumb. I hated seeing how happy he was. I didn't believe it. But now I know that that is who he really was.

Hope is funny. It will never let you down. You can even hope for the wrong thing, but if you trust, even the wrong thing will get you through. I waited my whole life for my mother to come and save me. I knew that one day she would appear and finally I would learn the truth and everything would be OK. And I guess that's what happened.

They're letting me out today. The guard just told me that the warden will be here in a minute. There's a cool breeze coming in through the window. It's been hot all week but today it got nice. I've been thinking all morning about those men milling around the lobby of the MGM waiting to see Neil Diamond. I can't get their faces out of my mind. Their faces changed when he sang to them. Something happened that I don't understand. Time stood still and their pasts fell away. That's it. Their pasts fell away. And for those few brief moments their faces glowed with hope and they were free.

There is so much that I want to say good-bye to, so much I want to leave behind. But I don't know how to do it. I don't know how to do it and that scares me. All I know is that in this moment I can feel the breeze blowing through my hair, it feels cool against my skin. I can feel my elbow sliding along the table trying to keep up with my pen. And I can feel myself beginning to cry. I cry because I know that in this moment I have nothing to fear. I cry because I know that in this moment I am among the free.

ACKNOWLEDGMENTS

Thank you to Ed Burke and Signey Warner-Watson for getting the manuscript to Molly Friedrich at the Aaron Priest Agency. Molly, thanks for being my omniscient narrator — I couldn't have asked for a better guide. Deepest gratitude to my editor, Sarah Burnes, for her intelligence, patience, and her very keen eye. Thank you to my friends Wayne Reynolds, Shelby Hiatt, and Brendan Schallert for their enthusiastic comments and encouragement on the early draft and to Ray Escudero of the Los Angeles FBI for the hours he spent with me discussing law enforcement procedure.